Beer With Me

Love's Brew Series

BLUE SAFFIRE

Perceptive Illusions Publishing
Bayshore, New York

Blue Saffire/Perceptive Illusions Publishing, Inc
PO BOX 5253
Bayshore, NY 11706
www.BlueSaffire.com

Ordering Information:
Quantity sales. Special discounts are available on quantity purchases by corporations, associations, and others. For details, contact the "Special Sales Department" at the address above.

Beer With Me/ Blue Saffire. -- 1st ed.
ISBN 978-1-941924-37-2

Find the one who loves you and your dreams.

–BLUE SAFFIRE

PREFACE

Just Dreaming

Jo

"This place has a way of making you feel … I don't know." I pause and lift my shoulders to my ears. "Like you can accomplish anything."

I sit with my palms planted behind me as Chance and I sit up in the loft above the barn. We've been hanging out talking. He and Hershel have been super nice since Mom and I arrived, but Chance has something about him that puts me at ease.

"Yeah, Spring Valley has a way of becoming a part of you. Making the impossible seem possible. I've sat right here dreaming up all the things I want to make happen in my life."

"What did you come up with?" I ask with a smile on my face.

"I don't think I'm leaving. Not for good. I want to raise my family here.

"Hershel doesn't want to run the place like I do. I think when it's mine, I plan to make it a destination. Like I was telling you before, I want to make it a retreat. Someplace people come to relax and enjoy Spring Valley," he replies.

"That sounds amazing. I wish I knew what I wanted so clearly."

"You don't have plans?"

"Not like yours. I mean, things are going well with Jarold. I haven't introduced him to Mom and Dad, but now that the divorce is final, I'm thinking that I should—"

"Jarold?"

"Yeah, that's my boyfriend. We've been dating for about a year. Anyway, things are going well with him, but my career is still growing and I'm trying to make sense of that. Jarold thinks I should find a backup plan.

"He doesn't think massage therapy will do much for my pockets. That's insane because I haven't even tapped into all my options with my career and I make great money," I say and roll my eyes.

"Let me ask you something. If there wasn't a Jarold. If you only had to think about you and your future, what would you do?"

I sigh. "I don't know." I poke my lip out and sag my shoulders.

"You said this place makes you feel like you can accomplish anything. Tell me what you feel like you can accomplish right now in this moment."

"Okay, Chance. I'm going to tell you my secrets, you better not laugh at me. I'm trusting you as a friend."

"Go on, shoot," he says and bumps my shoulder.

"I want to run my own business. I would love to have a spa of my own where people can come to reset and relax. I want it to provide luxury, but I also want everyone to be able to come and have a full experience.

"Self-care matters and I want my clients to feel and remember that. I want them to feel like they're coming to see family. Like that one aunt who takes care of everyone and makes sure they're okay," I gush as I see it all in my head.

"Like your mom. That's who she is for you and your sisters. At least that's how you make it sound."

"Yeah, like Mom. I want everyone to know what it's like to have someone who cares for you. Someone who always creates a safe place. Does that sound crazy?"

"Not at all. Have you told Jarold this?"

"No, I have only ever told Mel and JC. We've talked about wanting to be financially set before starting a family. However, whenever we have that talk it turns to the lack of stability in my career."

"Well, what does he do?"

"He's in school for engineering. He wants to go into building race cars."

"Sure, because there are plenty of opportunities there," he snorts.

I snicker and bump him with my shoulder. "Be nice."

"Do you want children?"

"Yes, I want it all. The kids, the house, the successful business. I watched my parents have successful careers. I know it's possible.

"I also watched their marriage come apart. I want to have balance in my life to avoid the pitfalls I watched them fall into.

"My husband should be my best friend. I want to grow old with him. I want to have the mutual respect my mom and dad still have for each other."

"And this Jarold guy, you think you can have all that with him?"

I release a heavy breath. "Maybe if I bring him here … this place is magic. Maybe if he comes here, he'll see it all like I can. This place would be amazing for a wedding destination."

"Yeah, that's not a bad idea. I can only hope that my future wife can see how perfect our lives could be right here. She could be or do anything she wants. I would take care of everything to make sure she and our children are safe and happy."

"And Aunty Jo will be right here to spoil them every chance she gets."

Chance scoffs. "Yeah, but their mother would have to see it all first."

I wrinkle my brows as the mood seems to change a bit. It could be the beers I've been drinking or the fact that I'm a bit tired. I've been working with Chance and Hershel to make sure Mom is surprised when Mel and JC arrive.

My phone rings and I see it's my friend Marty. I roll my eyes. Marty always has some gossip to share. I get ready to ignore the call until Chance gets up and speaks.

"I'll let you take that. I want to get my last rounds in before I head to bed. It was good talking to you. Have a good night."

"Oh, goodnight."

CHAPTER ONE

Taking a Chance

Chance

Five and a half weeks later …

I'm happy for Pop. I know Coral is going to love the new SUV. I can't begrudge my father for finding love again. I watched how he loved my mom and how he stayed by her side up until the very end.

My parents had the kind of love that inspired hope and joy. I think he's been lucky enough to find that again. Pop is a great father and man. He deserves nothing less. I can only hope to find that kind of love once.

"Your dad is so sweet," Jo says, pulling me from my musing.

We're sitting in the kitchen at the B&B. Everyone else has called it a night. I probably should too. The group of us went out to Sea View to do some sightseeing to give Pop and Coral time alone.

Knowing Pop had a big date planned for the two of them, the girls all opted to crash at the B&B tonight after we all hung out at Willowbrook. This place feels more like home than ever since they've all come into town.

I know I've settled into my roots and dreams for the future since Jo has arrived. Our talks have put a lot into perspective for me. It's why I've finally stepped up to tell Pop my ideas.

We have our first wedding event tomorrow. I have to say I'm excited about it. When I told Pop we needed to start new things to draw more business, I never thought I'd be involved in wedding planning.

It's been cool so far. I'm actually too wired to sleep, so when Jo wanted something other than beer, I brought her in here to make her some hot chocolate.

"Yeah, he's great. Your mom is awesome too."

"I can only dream of finding that for myself," she sighs.

"Jarold still showing up at your job?"

"Ugh, don't remind me. Unfortunately, yes. I'm starting to think about moving here permanently. I'm over all the drama."

"Really?"

"Yeah, I sort of like it here. Besides, I've never been this far away from my mom and I'm not sure I'm ready for that. Not after the accident."

"That makes sense. That sure did shake us all up. I can only imagine what that was like for you as her daughter."

"I remember being so small when Mel and JC came to live with us. They were sad and scared. Not knowing what was next for them.

"I'm an adult but I think I would be just as scared and lost without my mom. I admire her for asking herself what's next and then taking action. I think it's time I do the same."

"And you think what's next could be here?"

"Yeah, with each day it's starting to sound like a better idea. I have enough in savings to figure things out and not have to work for a while. I'd be staying with Mom so that will save me money."

"You could come work at the B&B while you figure things out. I wouldn't mind some help with events like this wedding. I'm sure Pop would agree."

"I wouldn't want to be a bother. I'll be fine. I really think I'm going to put in my two weeks' notice when I get back this week. That will line up with my next visit here."

I clear my throat and turn to face her. Her eyes have gone distant as if she's deep in thought. She's gorgeous.

It seems like she gets prettier with each day. There's this pull I feel toward her. I've never felt this with anyone else.

Sure, I've dated a lot, but no one has compared to Jo. She makes me feel at ease. Suddenly, her eyes come back into focus.

She gives me a smile as she finds me staring at her. Miss Coral's words ring in my head. If I want Jo to know how I feel, I have to be direct.

If she's moving here, that will be my chance. We can give this a go. I just need to make things clear.

"Do I have something on my face?"

She lifts her hand to wipe at her lip. I've fully committed to this course. I reach to palm the side of her face and lean in.

I lick my lips. "No, I just …" My words trail off as I crush my lips to hers in a searing kiss.

I groan as the flavor of caramel, spice, and chocolate hit my tongue. I feel like I'm on a high as we kiss passionately. Jo allows me to take over the kiss, and I deepen it.

She moans into my mouth, causing me to smile into the kiss. Something clatters to the floor in another room, and we pull apart. Well, Jo jumps back and drops her gaze to the floor.

I sit happy as a pig in slop. That kiss was better than I thought it would be. I go to lean in for another, but Jo jumps to her feet.

She wrings her hands in front of her as she will look anywhere but at me. I furrow my brows trying to figure out what's going on. She had to feel that. The chemistry between us is insane. That kiss …

"I … I … um, I should head up to bed. Thanks for the hot chocolate. Um, goodnight."

With that, she takes off running from me. I sit staring after her wondering what I did wrong.

"Fuck," I growl and shove my hands into my hair.

Jo

Oh my gosh. I can't believe Chance just kissed me. It was an amazing kiss. God is he a great kisser, but that's not us.

Chance and Hershel have been my friends from day one. However, I think I have a stronger bond with Chance. We've gotten deep during our talks. He knows so much about me.

That kiss could ruin everything. I don't want to date. I took a chance with Jarold, and he proved me right. I'm not meant to be in a relationship.

"Hey, you all right?" JC asks from the bed across from mine as I creep back into our suite.

Mel took the master bedroom since she's the oldest. Not that we didn't try to get it for ourselves. Mel has always been the older sister and there for the leader.

I never put up much of a fight. I was happy to have them come to live with us. They have always been my favorite people in the world.

"Yeah, I'm fine."

"Did that jerk call you again. Just block him already, Jo. You can do so much better."

"It's not about Jarold. I'm just ready to go home. I have a lot on my mind."

"Like wanting to open your own place. I think it's a great idea. Tell Mom or at least tell Uncle Ralph. Either of them will back you," she mutters and flips on her other side, so her back is to me and the light I turned on.

"If I tell them, they're going to want to help. I want to do this on my own. My parents can't always run to my rescue."

"Sometimes it's better to ask for help. It's not that we can't do it on our own. It's more so not needing to. Goodnight, Jo. I love you, sis."

"Love you too. Good night."

I finish undressing, wrap my hair, and go to brush my teeth. As I brush my teeth my mind wonders to the first time I met Chance. I had thought he was handsome initially, but I didn't think more of it as I already had a boyfriend.

"Oh, Mom, wait, I forgot my purse in the car," I said as we walked into the B&B to check in.

I turned to head back outside to retrieve my bag as no one was at the reception counter as we arrived. I grabbed my purse off the back seat of mom's car and remembered the bag I placed in the trunk.

"Might as well get that while I'm at it," I murmured to myself.

"Hey, you need a hand with that?" I jumped startled and dropped my purse. "I'm sorry about that. Here, let me help."

I turned to find a guy with a baseball cap on. He picked up my purse and handed it to me. Then he picked up my bag and closed the trunk for me.

"Oh, thank you. You don't have to worry about that. I can carry it."

I had my hair washed and set for this trip. It had fallen into my eyes as I was startled. I combed it out of my view and looked up at him.

His smile grew as his gaze bounced over my face. He took his hat off and I could fully see his face. My lips parted a little.

Wow, he's handsome. His eyes were a pretty blue and his hair was thick and dark. He had the perfect nose for his face, and his lips were a rosy pink and had a fullness about them that complimented his face.

He could totally be a model if he wanted. That smile was worth money. The little mole on the right side of his face right over his lip was cute. As was the dimple in his left cheek.

Teen movie heart throb much? I remembered having crushes on guys like him as I watched TV when I was younger. My boyfriend now was the total opposite.

Jarold is tall dark and handsome. He's smart, driven, and I think he'll be the one someday. Speaking of which, I needed my purse for my phone so I could call Jarold once I got up to my room.

"No, I've got it. Are you here to check in for a stay?"

"Yeah, me and my mom. She's here for the librarian job in town. I was so excited to check in, I forgot my purse."

"I'm Chance. I run this place with my brother and my dad. Let me know if you need anything, I'll be happy to help."

I shake my head clear as I come back to the present. So much has changed from that day. I rinse my mouth out and head back into the bedroom to climb into bed.

Why would he kiss me? This could make things so complicated. I thought he liked being my friend.

Oh God, all the time he spends with me. Could I have been reading things wrong all this time? This can't be happening.

CHAPTER TWO

Lonely

Jo

I poke my fork at the beef fried rice in my carton. I'm eating alone again. Mel and JC work long hours and are hardly ever here. I miss Mom.

I used to come over, and we would have dinner together. Now that she lives in Spring Valley and I've moved back here, it doesn't feel the same. It doesn't feel like the house I grew up in.

My phone rings on the island top and I look to see the caller is my best friend, Marty. Marty and I met in junior high school. He was shy and kept to himself a lot.

I never stuck to one friend group, so when Marty said something funny under his breath in gym, I made it my business to become his friend. From that day he's been one of my biggest cheerleaders.

It's odd because I don't allow people to get too close, but Marty has always been there. I guess, once we became friends, he wasn't willing to allow me to push him away. Over the years, I've made my peace with that, but I still haven't let him in too close.

"Hey, what's up?"

"I'm calling to see if you're in wonderland or if you're back here on earth with the rest of us. I miss you."

"I'm home. Mom is doing better, and I needed to come home to sort my own life out."

"You sound off. What's going on? I hope you're not thinking about getting back with that asshole."

"Not at all." I roll my eyes. "He has sent me roses at work twice this week. And still, I have too much on my mind to even care."

"What's on your mind, friend?"

"Chance kissed me, and I ran," I say in almost a whisper.

"Wait, slowdown and back that up for me."

"You remember I told you about my friends Hershel and Chance?"

"Yes, yes, the rancher, brewer, hotties with the blue eyes. I remember but that's not what I'm trying to process. You said one of them kissed you?"

"Yeah, the younger brother kissed me. Chance. I feel so stupid. I got up and ran."

"Was it that bad? Did he try to force himself on you?"

"Not at all. He's an amazing kisser. He made … he made my toes curl in my shoes, and I had a heartbeat in my … Oh, never mind."

"So what's the problem?"

"I don't date."

"Hello, and that's my point right there. And why not? You're effortlessly gorgeous, you're twenty-three and have a great clientele, making your career successful."

"That alone is a problem. Chance is twenty-seven. What does he want with me?"

"Um, let me see. Maybe to go on a date or two. Get to know you."

"He has his family's legacy to work on. I'm still trying to find my way."

"Jo, I need you to be honest with me because your reasons for not dating have never made sense to me."

"They make sense to me. Chance doesn't need me in his life as more than a friend."

"You're always so willing to throw a good thing away. Why did you give Jarold a chance?"

I shrug as if he can see me. "I think I always knew it wouldn't work. I just needed to prove something to myself."

"And what's that?"

"Honey, I'm home," Mel sings through the house as she comes in.

"Hey, I have to go. I'll call you later."

Chance

"Hey, you. You want a slice of this pie?" Miss Coral asks as I find her humming and smiling in the kitchen at the B&B.

She and Pop are getting really serious. If Pop isn't at Willowbrook, the two are here. I like having her around. Her smile alone is good for the soul.

"Nah, I'm trying to watch my figure," I say and pat my belly.

Coral snickers. "If I hear one more person say that. None of you have a true ounce of fat to begin with.

"However, I'll admit JC is making life hard for us all around here. Why do you think I brought this pie over here to share?"

"I don't think a one of us minds. Her food is made with love. You mind if I sit with you while you eat?"

"Sure, why not? Although, I would think a handsome young man like you would rather be out on a date with a young lady his own age," she teases.

"No, ma'am. I haven't been lucky in love lately. I think it's best I focus on something else."

"Ut-oh. Does this have anything to do with Jo?"

I sigh and look down at the table in front of me. I haven't been able to get that kiss off my mind. Jo was with me.

I know I wasn't the only one who felt something. The sparks were there. She kissed me back.

"Yes, ma'am. It sort of does. I messed up."

"How so?"

"I kissed Jo. She ran right after and was gone the next morning without saying a word. I usually pack her things in her car for her, but she was gone. I thought she was going to at least stick around for the wedding and everything."

Coral sighs. "Jodie may be an only child, but she's been raised like the youngest of three. I blame myself. I wanted my sister's children to feel welcomed and loved.

"I gave them a ton of attention in the beginning and then I noticed a change in Jo so I might have smothered her and babied her too much as a result.

"Jo seems like she's always trying to find her own way. She'll see something she wants, and she'll take the long way around it trying to please everyone else.

"Sometimes you have to show her there's a better way and then allow her to take that path on her own. Do you get what I mean? It can be a lot of work, but if you think she's worth it—which as her mother I think she is—you will find yourself rewarded when she finds you were what she wanted all along."

"Yeah, but how do I know she wants me? She ran," I murmur.

"Again, I'm her mother. I've seen the way Jo looks at you. She may not realize it yet, but she's smitten with you."

I give a smile. "I'm pretty crazy about her."

"Then show her the way, Chance. After you show her, allow her to find her way there."

I look into Coral's eyes searching until it clicks. I know just what I plan to do. If I want Jo, I need to show her what it would be like to be here with me.

"Okay, thanks. You mind if I take off. I have some planning I want to do."

She gives me a huge smile. "You go right ahead and good luck."

"Thank you, ma'am."

I jump to my feet with renewed energy. There's so much I need to get done. I'll have to talk to Pop in the morning about my plan.

CHAPTER THREE

Can We Talk

Jo

I rub the back of my neck and roll my shoulders. It's been a long day. I'm always drained after Mrs. Lawson's sessions.

The woman comes in with enough knots and tension for two people. The way she talks about her husband, I can see why. He sounds like a creep but she's staying with him for the money.

That's something I respect about my mom. She never allowed money to make decisions for her. Mom has always been one to make her own money.

I learned how to save and grow my money from her. Sure, Dad has taught me a thing or two, but Mom is the reason I have a nice nest egg I created on my own.

Me and my sisters are all well off. The three of us have joked about quitting our jobs to travel the world together. I know it's a joke because Mel is a workaholic and JC is a bit of a control freak.

She wouldn't be able to leave behind all the hard work she's done for the non-for-profit she works for. I, on the other hand, am ready for change.

At twenty-three, I feel like something is missing. To be honest, now that things are over between Jarold and me, I can see we weren't a fit. As hard as I tried, I couldn't let him in.

I just haven't dug too deeply into that because it could debunk my other beliefs and give me false hope. If what I know is true, I'll only hurt the one I'm supposed to love.

"Hey, Jo," Bell says as she comes into the back room.

I turn to give her a smile. Bell and I have been friends for years before she left for college to pursue an art degree. She came back and started working here about a year ago.

"Hey, Bell. What's up?"

"Same old, same old. I need a night out. You haven't been around much lately and those other trolls I hang with have been on some bullshit.

"You have to save me. I need to decompress with good people. Not fear I'm going to be stuck with the bill or left in the club with no way home because one of my asshole friends left to hook up with some guy and took my purse with her," Bell whines.

"I still can't believe that one. That was such a dick move."

"Ugh, I haven't spoken to her since. She's really mad at me about it too."

"Unbelievable. I've been going back and forth between the city and my mother's new place. I wasn't going to go back this weekend, so maybe we can hang or something."

"Shit, my sister's wedding is this weekend. How about next weekend?"

"I'm not sure about my plans yet. I'll keep you posted."

"Oh, by the way. Karen said to tell you your boyfriend was here. He was sitting out front waiting for you again."

I roll my eyes and groan. Jarold keeps showing up here trying to get me to talk to him. I have nothing to say to him.

The time for a conversation between us has passed. He needs to back off and respect my space and work. I can't have him stalking me at my job around my clients.

"Gah, he's my ex-boyfriend. Why won't he leave me alone?"

"You never did tell me what's going on with that situation. You want me to call my cousins to handle him? He won't bring his butt back here again after they're done."

I laugh, knowing she means it. Bell has always had my back. In high school, she wouldn't allow anyone to mess with me.

"No, it's fine. I'll handle it. When we go out for drinks, I'll fill you in on everything," I say.

"Oh, that's my next client. I'll call you later," Bell sings as she rushes to give me a hug.

I return the hug before I release her and go back to finishing up so I can clock out and head home. My mind wonders to Chance. A week ago, I would have texted him after I got off work and we would have talked during my ride home.

Now, I'm going to get some ice cream and head home to surf the net. Maybe I should take some time to look over my business plan. I shake that thought off and collect my things to leave.

"See you tomorrow," I say and wave bye to Nisha the receptionist as I head out the front door.

I'm digging through my purse for my car keys as I get out into the parking lot. Suddenly, someone walks up and grabs my arm. I drop my bag to my side and start to swing it.

"Jo, Jo, I just want to talk to you. Damn, can you stop hitting me."

"Jarold? Ugh, what don't you get? I don't want to talk to you," I snarl.

"Shit, I'm going to have a fucking knot. What's in that thing?"

"You're lucky that's all you got. Next time I pistol whip you it will be with a naked Glock."

"Listen, baby. I just want to talk."

"I'm not your baby and we have nothing to talk about. You can leave and stop coming around here before you get me written up or fired," I snap.

"I'm going to keep coming until you talk to me. We had something. I want—"

I scoff. "Nah, boo. That's your problem. You're worried about what you want. You never once stopped to think about me.

"I'm doing you a favor. You don't have to worry about me at all. You can do whatever you like now, and you don't have to worry about me one bit. Goodbye."

With that, I turn and climb into my car. He stands in front of my car glaring at me like he's not going to move. I rev the engine a few times to warn him he's not as crazy as he thinks but I am.

When he still doesn't move, I shift the car into drive. He jumps out of the way just in time. I groan as I find my boss standing outside the spa watching on.

"Why me?" I mutter to myself. "Looks like that decision has been made for me."

I'm moving to Spring Valley. There's no way I can show my face at work again. All I have to do is stay away from Chance.

That should be easy, right? Gah, fuck my life.

Chance

"Hey, Chance, it's good to see you. I was so happy you called," Lena says as I walk into Shelby's to meet her for coffee.

"Hey, Lena. Thanks for meeting me on such short notice. I wanted to keep the business local, and you were the first person I thought of."

I know how much the local businesses need the patronage in order for all the planning and hard work Cash and the ladies have been doing to have an effect, I called Lena. She wasn't my first choice, but she seemed like the right one when it came to what Spring Valley needs. Besides, she knows me.

"Well, I thank you for the business and for thinking of me. What's your daddy up to now?"

"It's actually not Pop this time. It's for me."

"For you? What do you have in mind?"

"I want to build my forever home, but since Mama ain't here anymore, I need a woman's touch on the design. You know, someone to tell me what my wife would like in a home," I say as my cheeks burn.

"Oh, and your daddy's new girlfriend doesn't want to help?"

"Well, it's sort of a surprise. I don't want too many people to know before it's done. You know how news flies around here.

"I want to have the place done before I tell her it's hers or that I want her to live there with me. I mean, I'm sure I'll be able to ask Miss Coral for her input once the place is ready, but for now, I was hoping you could help me design the perfect place for a young couple.

"Pop has agreed to let me build not far from Willowbrook. He's digging up the blueprints for that house, and I thought you could help me personalize them."

"I would absolutely love to. Willowbrook is such a gorgeous property. I didn't know you were dating.

"She's one lucky gal. I can't wait to meet her," she says as she searches my face.

"Well, that's the thing. We're not dating. Not right now, but I know she's the one. I just need a chance to show her how good we are together, and I know it's all going to fall into place.

"I figure it will take some time to build the place. That gives me plenty of time to make things right and get us to where we need to be. By the time the house is done, I'll have a ring and all."

"Oh, this is going to be so much fun," Lena says excitedly. "I already have so many ideas. I know exactly what I would want if someone did this for me."

She gives me a wink. However, I turn my attention to Alice as she comes over with coffee and my favorite fudge. My stomach settles as I have someone to help me with this task.

It should take me six months to a year to get the house done. I'm sure I can win Jo over by then. If I don't, she'll have a house of her own next door to her mama as a gift from me.

Sitting back in my chair, I smile as I feel more confident than I have in a while. That spark was there. I just need time to show Jo we belong together.

I'm her man whether she knows it or not. I have a plan and I'm sticking to it. I'm building for our future.

"It's been a while since I've seen you two in here together. Can I get you anything else?" Alice says.

"Not today, Alice. I want to get back to the ranch to do some more planning. I have a lot to get in order," I say and give Lena a wink.

I also picked Lena because she's always been private and big on her client's privacy. When we were in school together, she didn't run around town telling everyone anyone's business. I can't say that about a lot of the others in our circle. Male or female.

This is going to be awesome.

CHAPTER FOUR

A Little Help

Jo

I've been in Spring Valley for two weeks since the incident with Jarold. I put in my resignation before Felicia could fire me, which from the look on her face she was ready to do.

Mom hasn't pushed after I told her I'm taking a break to figure somethings out. She welcomed me with open arms. However, today I've noticed the way she's been looking at me.

I thought I would be able to avoid her watchful eye since she has returned to work. Not a chance. This is Coral Marks I'm talking about.

I've been out back sitting by the fire to avoid her since she got home from work. I'm hoping Jack will show up soon to get her attention off me. To be honest, she's been more watchful since game night when Jack gave her the new car.

I did my best to avoid Chance that night. However, that sort of pulled a few peoples' attention. Mel and JC asked me about it after the fact.

"Oh, you're reading that series. I loved it. You have to let me know what you think about it," Mom says as I place my e-reader down to pick up my hot chocolate for a sip.

"This is my second time reading it. I loved the entire series," I gush.

Mom's eyes light up. "Yes, one of my favorites. It would be a perfect choice for book club."

"Are we going to start back up? I have a few suggestions. I can't believe how lucky I've been lately to find so many good reads back-to-back."

"I've been wanting to start the club back up. I was thinking about putting up a few feelers at the library," she says excitedly.

"I'm ready when you are."

"All right. I'll get the ball rolling. It will be a nice way for you to meet more people your own age too."

"Meet some people her age? Why don't you introduce her to a few of your friends, Chance?" Jack croons as he and Chance come out of the house.

I stifle a groan as I look anywhere but at Chance. There's nowhere for me to run. I can feel his eyes locked on me.

In this moment, I wish the ground would open up and swallow me. I hate this awkward feeling. In the past, I used to be ready to jump up and head in the house to watch a movie with Chance as soon as he arrived.

Now, I'll do anything to keep from being left alone with him. I glance at Mom out the corner of my eye and catch her watching me closely. I clear my throat and get ready to excuse myself.

"I'd love to introduce you to my circle. I can't believe we haven't hung out with the gang yet. I can text to see what's up tonight," Chance says.

"Sounds good. You should go get ready, Jo," Mom says.

"I don't know. Chance isn't really my age, meaning all his friends are older than me. If the goal is to find me more friends my age, I don't think he'll be much help.

"I was thinking of staying in and surfing the net to research some of my ideas. Thanks, but no thanks," I murmur.

"Oh, come on. It will be fun. Some of my friends have younger siblings that hang with us. Besides, your mature for your age.

"You'll fit right in. Dustin says they're all heading to the bar tonight. Luke's is a great spot. Good music and some axe throwing," Chance says with a smile.

"Oh, that does sound fun," Mom sings. "Come on, Jo. I'll give you some money if that's what you're worried about."

"What? No, I don't need your money, Mom. I just ..." I sigh.

The look in Mom's eyes tells me this is a losing battle. I might as well go and get dressed. She's not going to let up until I do.

"I'll be ready in about twenty," I say to Chance.

"I'll be right here waiting. Take your time."

Chance

I grin at Pop and Coral as I take the seat Jo just vacated. I rode over with Pop, hoping I would be able to get a chance to talk to Jo. She's been avoiding me since she got in about two weeks ago.

I've just been too busy with my plans to corner her and find out what's going on. Other than game night, this is the first time I'm getting to focus on something other than the ranch.

I didn't want to ruin Pop's night when he gave Coral the new truck, so I never got to confront Jo then. Pop winks at me as he sits next to Coral. I appreciate the two trying to help me.

I do know why I never took Jo around my friends. I've wanted her all to myself. It's bad enough Hershel had been interested in her.

The guys already had a ton of questions after the festival. I blew them all off and told them she didn't live here so they were wasting their time. It wasn't a lie at the time.

However, now that it seems she's moving here it would be nice for her to make some friends who will make her want to have roots here. Dawn and Ginger will make her feel welcome.

This could be good. Jo has this light about her. It makes you want to bask in it and be near her.

I begin to get excited as I wait for Jo to return. Everything seems to be falling into place. This was meant to be. I can feel it in my gut.

"Okay, I'm ready," Jo says, causing me to look up from my phone.

It's been about twenty minutes. Pop and Coral have been talking and laughing amongst themselves as if I'm not even here. My mouth falls open as my eyes land on Jo.

Her outfit is simple but she's taking my breath away. I can't help the smile that comes to my lips. She has on a cute light blue sundress and a denim jacket.

The espadrilles on her feet give her a little height and make her brown legs look long and silky. Her hair is down and frames her pretty face. Clearing my throat, I get to my feet.

"You look great," I breathe as I move to her side.

"Thanks."

CHAPTER FIVE

Oh No

Coral

I moan and dig my nails into Jack's back as he rocks into me. Each time I think our love making can't get any more passionate, he takes it to a new level.

"Coral," he groans into my ear.

"Oh my God, yes. Right there. I'm going to come."

He grunts loudly and reaches between us to pinch my clit. My eyes roll back, and I pull my legs back farther into my chest. Jack slips in deeper and hardens more.

"Fuck, woman. You feel so good. I can't get enough of you and this tight pussy. If I were twenty years younger, I'd put a baby in you.

"I want to connect to you in every way, baby girl. I love you so much. Go on and come, I'm right there with you," he groans.

His words sink in, and I'm touched. I'm not having any more children at my age, but I understand what he means. This connection between us is ever growing.

"Jack, yes," I cry out as I begin to convulse around him as I feel him spill into me.

It's hot and feels like so much as he pumps a few more times. Right as he rolls onto his back, his cell phone rings. He reaches for it as he wipes the sweat from his face.

"Hello?" he says breathlessly.

Jo

I'd be lying if I said I didn't have a good time with Chance and his friends. Although I did use his friends as buffers throughout the night. I have to admit Chance didn't push.

I appreciate that. I was able to have fun without feeling awkward or wanting to leave. I like Dawn, Tammy, Ginger, and Ann. I can see myself hanging out with them again some time. They've already invited me out with them for a girls' night.

The guys were cool as well, but I got the feeling Chance wasn't too happy when Beck kept trying to talk to me. Beck is nice but not my type. There's a difference between confidence and arrogance.

Seeing Chance with his friends, revealed a quiet confidence about him that I never took notice of before. I guess that's why I'm so comfortable around him. Chance is comfortable in his skin and easy to get along with.

We have the same tastes in movies and food. He gets my humor and he's pretty funny himself. I've spent the night thinking about all the things I like about Chance which has reminded me why this is a bad idea.

"I told you they would love you. Did you have a good time?" Chance asks, breaking into my thoughts as we head back to the ranch.

"I did. They were all very nice. Thank you for taking me along."

"You're welcome. Anytime. There were a few of the crew missing but you should get to meet everyone next time."

Ignoring his comment about next time, I clear my throat and look out of the window on the passenger's side. "You're good at axe throwing. It was fun to watch everyone try."

"You did pretty good yourself. I'd be happy to give you a few pointers."

"Does the bar get their beer from you guys?"

"No," he sighs. "Listen, Jo. I'm sorry about that kiss. I didn't mean to make things awkward between us.

"I just … I. I can't be the only one who feels this thing between us. You're so gorgeous and I want to be around you all the time.

"I miss you when you're not here. I … I thought if I kissed you, I'd be putting it out there how I've been feeling about you," he stammers.

"Chance, it's not you. You're a really nice guy—"

Suddenly there's a loud hissing sound and the truck begins to slow down. Chance groans and starts to pull over to the side of the road. This can't be happening.

"Wh … what's going on?"

"I don't know yet. Can you hand me the flashlight from the glove compartment?"

I get the flashlight and hand it over to him. He's already on his phone as he climbs out of the truck. I hope he's calling Hershel or Jack.

It's really dark out there. I unfasten my seatbelt and scoot to the edge of my seat as I wring my hands. When he lefts the hood and smoke bellows out, my heart sinks.

I climb out of the truck and go to stand by him to see if I can hold the flashlight or something. When his face comes into view, he has a frown on his lips, and his brows are knit. He's gorgeous.

Once again, I think of how much he looks like a movie star or model like the first time I saw him. My mind goes to that kiss.

I want nothing more than to lean in and connect our lips. He lifts his gaze to mine and I take a step back and clear my throat. Quickly, I dart my eyes away not wanting him to see my reaction to him.

"Hersh isn't answering his phone. I can fix it, but I'll need him to bring me a couple of things from the barn. It's gotten cold out here. You want to get back in the truck?

"I'll keep calling to see if he'll pick up. As a last resort, I'll call Pop. I think I have some blankets inside to help keep you warm."

"I'm fine. I think all the alcohol in my system is helping out at the moment," I say with a smile.

He moves in closer and crowds my space, placing his hands on my hips. "Are you sure? It gets pretty cool at night this time of year. I'd hate for you to catch a cold."

I clear my throat and take a step back. "I … I think we both should get inside where it's safe. It's kind of dark out here."

"Okay, come on," he says and walks me to the passenger side to open the door for me.

I climb in and sit nervously as he rounds the truck to get back in behind the wheel. When he gets back in, he reaches to turn the music on. I peek out the corner of my eye and find him watching me.

"This will give us some time to talk," he murmurs.

"Or we could sit in silence while we wait for help, right?"

He snorts. "I don't get you, Jo. I've been flirting with you since day one. When I found out you were seeing someone, I backed off and became your friend.

"You're single now and there's this crazy attraction between us. Why are you fighting it? Don't you want to see where this could go?"

"Chance, I am attracted to you but … I just think this is a bad idea. My mom and your dad are dating. I'm new to town.

"I have so much to figure out right now, and dating will only complicate that. I like hanging out with you, can't we leave it at that?"

"Pop and your mom don't give two squats about what we do or don't do. They only care that we're happy. It doesn't have to be complicated if we don't want it to be.

"I like hanging out with you too, but why can't we give us a try. We fit, Jo. We make a whole lot of sense together."

"Yeah, Chance, you say that now, but I … just forget it," I huff and turn away.

I don't tell him we can't because I'll ruin everything. Saying it's not you, it's me sounds lame. If I tell him that, he'll want me to dig into those wounds to reveal why, and I've never done that with anyone.

"Hello, Pop. I'm so sorry to bother you but I can't get in touch with Hershel, and my truck broke down. I need a few things to get her back up and running."

CHAPTER SIX

New Build

Chance

It's been a month since Jo and I broke down on the side of the road. I've decided to back off for now and try another approach. I don't want to pressure her if she's not ready to date.

She did just break up with her boyfriend after all. I need to demonstrate some patience. Never been my strong suit but I'm capable.

I've been keeping plenty busy with the house and the B&B. Dad's been giving me more and more responsibilities. It's starting to feel right.

Things with the house are coming together as well. Lena has had some great ideas. Although she has gotten frustrated with me when I've decided against some of her suggestions, I know Jo wouldn't like.

She's still after me about the placement of a few of the windows. Jo loves natural lighting and where I had the windows drawn up in our house will give her the best lighting. Lena has argued it would be too much and would take way from wall space for hanging pictures and mirrors.

All things I know Jo wouldn't care much about. I'm not going to budge no matter how much Lena pushes back on it, that's one of the reasons we're meeting today at Harbors'.

Antonio has drawn up some 3D designs for me to look at with different lighting options. I want Lena to see that I don't care what designs they come up with, I'm not changing my mind.

She needs to get that in her head now. According to her, I need to make final decisions as the boys and I will be installing windows and doors in a few weeks. Things have been moving fast.

"This is a nice kitchen. I've always said Harbors' has some of the best designs for a smalltown business and all," Lena says as she walks up and hands me an ice coffee.

"Thanks," I say as I take the cup.

"I got it just how you like it. Not too sweet with two shots of caramel. Some things you never forget," she chimes as she looks up at me with a bright smile.

I take a sip and try not to frown. I hate this shit. I like my coffee hot and it's with three pumps of caramel, heavy on the espresso.

"I took a few pictures of some things I think would be nice in the house. I'll share them with you later. Antonio said to let him know when you arrived."

She places a hand on my bicep. "Lead the way. I can't wait for him to show you the concepts I sent over. You're going to totally see what I mean when he brings it all to life."

"I'm sure whatever he has will be fine enough, I'm just not going to change the plan for those windows. I want the natural lighting. Especially the skylight balcony.

"That one is important to me. That room is going to be my little girl's playroom. I want to sit in there on rainy days or starry nights and help her dream up her future. The bookshelves, the window, the secret passageway, that's all for my girls," I say.

"Wow, I didn't know that was what you were thinking. That's so sweet. Maybe we'll leave that one in, but you have to listen to me with the other parts of the house. Isn't that what a partnership is all about?"

"Hey, there you guys are. Just give me a minute to help Miss Coral and Jo here and I'll be right with you for those designs," Antonio calls out.

I turn to find Jo looking at me with her lips pursed in a tight line. I take a step away from Lena and rub my hands on my thighs as they suddenly begin to sweat. Before I can say anything, Jo turns and walks away.

"Hey, Chance. How are you?" Miss Coral asks.

"I'm good, ma'am. Just here looking at some designs for a project I'm working on. Let me introduce you to the designer helping me out. This is Lena. We went to school together.

"If you ever need something done at the house, she's the local designer. Lena, this is Miss Coral. Pop's girlfriend," I say.

"Hello, it's nice to meet you. I've heard so much about you. You're the new librarian, am I correct?"

"You are. That was my daughter, Jo. We're looking for some new drapes for her bedroom. Jack said this is the place to come for home anything," Coral says with a smile.

"That it is but if you ever want any help with anything I'd be happy to come on in with you," Lena says politely.

"If you'll excuse me for a minute," I say to Lena before I take off to follow Jo.

Jo

I feel so stupid for being jealous. I practically pushed Chance away. I didn't expect him to wait around for me, and he doesn't owe me anything, but it still stings to see him with someone else.

She's pretty and looks more like what I expect him to go after. I think what bothers me the most is the way she looked at Chance and the fact that they are here in a home design store. Hershel may have let it slip that Chance has been working on building his own house.

I mean, you can't miss all the building going on across the way from Mom's, but I just recently found out that it's going to be Chance's home. Is he building it for them? For her?

How long have they been dating? I should be happy for them. Maybe now Chance and I can go back to the friendship we once had.

While I feel a pang of sadness, I also feel a bit of happiness to know I can have that friend back. I hope.

When Chance and I were hanging out, I was able to see my future more clearly. He asked the right questions to make me think and make decisions. With him, I'm always honest with myself.

I'm not looking to spare his feelings or please him for fear he'll be upset with me. At least that was before. I would love to have that back.

"Penny for your thoughts."

I startle and jump as Chance speaks into my ear. I had been so lost in my head; I didn't notice him come up behind me. I turn to face him, and he searches my face with his gaze.

"I'm just looking at these drapes. I love the color, but I would have to change so much for them to work. I don't want to make that many changes. The room already has such a beautiful vibe," I say.

"You know, change isn't always a bad thing. Sometimes we have to take the leap first to find where we fit. You can always make something your own when you remember who you are at your core.

"The change is to the environment surrounding not the central existence. Sometimes a change of scenery is all that's needed to bring comfort to the overall situation," he says.

"I miss our talks," I blurt out. "Maybe that's wrong of me to say since you're dating someone now and I'm sorry if it comes off that way, but I do miss talking to you."

He snorts a laugh. "Lena? You think I'm dating Lena? Jo, she and I went to school together. She's helping me with a project.

"I'm still very single and I miss our talks too. I miss coming to Willowbrook and sitting under a blanket while watching movies with you. I miss our trips to the barn to drink beer and bullshit.

"I wish you would tell me how to fix what I fucked up because I'm so miserable without you. I'd like to have my best friend back. Will you have a playdate with me?"

I burst into laughter as I nod. "I would like that. Can your dad bring you over later? I'll make us some popcorn."

We used to joke that our movie days together were our playdates while Jack would come over to visit Mom. I believe Jack didn't want people to see his truck sitting at Mom's all day and night so he would ride with Chance to keep the rumors at bay. It's always been a nice gesture and it's how Chance and I really started to bond.

He gives me a big smile. "I'll make sure all my chores are done and I'll bring the beer."

"Sounds awesome. I think you're right. I'm going to go with these. There's something cheerful about them. Thanks."

"Anytime, Sunshine."

Lena

I get in my car and want to scream. Chance was totally unfocused after he went to talk to that girl. Not to mention he totally shut down my ideas to axe those windows.

I don't want that much natural lighting in my home. We'll have to add blinds to all those window just not to feel like we're in a fish bowl or some type of exhibit.

Taking a deep breath, I try to think of what to do next. I can't allow anything to take this opportunity from me. Chance knows as well as I do that we make a good thing.

"Hey, Dawn, what can you tell me about that Jo girl?"

"You mean Miss Coral's daughter?"

"Yeah, the librarian's daughter. What do you know about her?"

"She's pretty cool. I like her. Chance brought her out to Luke's one night and we all got to hang. I think that was when you went to get your hair done in Levyville.

"You know, for that guy you said you were getting back together with. How's that working out? Did he actually propose?"

"We're taking things slow. I don't want to rush him into anything. Right now, I'm just trying to make sure he isn't distracted or anything," I reply.

"Distracted? What do you mean?"

"It's nothing. Everything is going as it should. He still has that big gift he's working on for me. Have you guys hung out since?"

"Who? Jo?"

"Yeah."

"No, we were supposed to get together but everyone's schedules haven't been able to sync up. That reminds me. I meant to give her a call to see if she wants to hang out one on one.

"It doesn't have to be everyone. Thanks for the reminder. I'll give her a call when we hang up."

"Do you mind if I come along. I would like to get to know her."

"I ... uh ... well, you're seeing someone, right? You've given up on that thing you had for Chance?"

It wasn't a thing I had for Chance. I hate that she makes it seem like it was a one-sided thing. Our timing was just bad.

I did something stupid, and it all got fucked up. Things are different now. There's nothing in my way and Chance doesn't know about the past.

CHAPTER SEVEN

The Pull is Strong

Chance

Don't fuck this up. Don't fuck this up. Don't fuck this up.

I've been chanting those words in my head for hours. Jo smells so good and her simple ponytail and loungewear are driving me crazy. She looks so darn adorable.

"Oh, this is my favorite part. I've watched this movie a million times and it never gets old."

"I love the way your eyes light up when you're talking about your favorite movies or a book you love. You should totally have a movie room in your home.

"I could see you and your family hanging out in there making all sorts of fun memories. Your favorite movies on hidden shelves even though you already have them loaded up digitally," I say as I allow my eyes to bounce over her face.

"Oh my God, that would be so awesome. There would be a popcorn machine and a kitchen right outside the theater where JC could bake everyone their favorite snacks. Oh, and coolers for all the beer my best friend would deliver to my house once a month," she snickers.

"As long as you have a grill right outside the sliding doors for me to come in and out through when I barbeque for the gang and I'd also be able to deliver the beer through that entrance." I shrug.

"Mm, good idea. I'll have to jot down some notes. I would love to do what you're doing some day. You know, build my own place. You're so lucky."

"You know I'm building a house?"

"Well, duh. It's right across the way. Hershel may have let it slip that it's your house."

I've never wanted to punch my brother in the face more. Why would he tell her it's my house? If it fucks this up, I'm kicking his ass.

She continues, pulling me from my thoughts. "I think it's cool. You said that's what you wanted. Now you're making it happen. Have you talked to your dad about the B&B? Will you be making those changes you talked about?"

"Yeah, we talked. I've already been working on a lot of the smaller things. Pop told me to write up a proposal and get back to him with it.

"I'm almost done. I've just been looking up supporting data to make sure it will all be lucrative."

"That's great, Chance. I'm so proud of you. I can only hope to start getting my life in order soon," she says and looks down into her lap, the movie now forgotten.

"What's stopping you?"

"Well, I guess I did take step one. I quit my job but what's next is the huge question."

"Then let's answer that right now. What's next, Jo?"

She looks me in my eyes and stares silently for a moment. There's that pull between us. It's like a pulse in the air. I want to lean in and take her lips so bad.

Don't fuck this up. Don't fuck this up. Don't fuck this up.

The chanting in my head is silenced as Jo cups my face and leans in to capture my lips. I groan into her mouth and take over the kiss immediately. It's even better than the first time.

"Jo, are you sure?" I break the kiss to ask.

"No, but yes. I'm going with how I feel. Tonight, it feels right to do this," she breathes before pressing her lips to mine once again.

I cup the side of her face and deepen the kiss. Just when I can't seem to get enough of her, she pushes me back and straddles my lap, allowing me access to get my hands on her body.

"I want you so much," I groan into her mouth.

"Oh my God, Chance. You're setting my body on fire."

"I'm just getting started, darlin'," I say as I kiss my way down her neck.

Reaching beneath her shirt, I palm her cute little breasts. They're not tiny and they're not huge. They're perfect for her body and to fit in the palms of my hands.

I'm already hard as hell but then she begins to grind into my lap. I can't believe this is happening. Warning bells in the back of my head tell me I should slow down, maybe leave and revisit this tomorrow.

We have both been drinking. I pull back and open my mouth to tell her what's on my mind, but she silences me as she pulls her shirt up and over her head. Her tits come into view and my mouth waters.

She's so fucking beautiful. When she stands and drops her sleep pants to the floor, I nearly burst from my pants. Oh shit, I'm going to fuck the shit out of that little pussy.

"Come to my room. Mom texted that she's staying with Jack tonight, but I don't want to do this here on her couch."

I nod, unable to find my words. She bends to pick up her things and turns to head to her room. I jump up as I watch her fat little ass and thick thighs sway.

"Fuck, you're mine and I can't wait to be inside you," I murmur to myself.

I work on the buttons of my shirt as I follow her to her room. Once inside, she drops her things and turns to face me. I tug off my shirt quickly and get to work on my jeans.

My shoes are already off as everyone takes their shoes off when they arrive. I shove my jeans and boxers down and kick them aside.

Once I'm completely naked, I widen my stance and straighten for her to take me in. Her eyes grow wide as she looks me over. My cock is so hard it's pointing at her.

"Oh my God, you're gorgeous all over," Jo gasps then laughs as she covers her mouth as if she didn't mean to say that.

Taking a few steps closer, I then reach for her waist and tug her to me. I take her lips in another searing kiss as I reach between her legs and find her wet seam.

She moans into my mouth and lifts up on her toes as I devour her mouth. While I rub her pussy, I use my other hand to explore her curves. Her skin is so soft.

"You're so wet. I want to taste you. Do you have any preferences?"

She pulls away and blinks up at me. "What do you mean?"

"How do you like to be fucked? Do you want to ride my face, or do you prefer sniper style? How do you want me to please you?"

"Chance, I … um … I." She swallows hard.

"You don't know. You've never had sex before."

She shakes her head shyly and looks away. I reach for her chin and bring her gaze back to mine. She has no idea, in this moment, I cherish her more than ever.

"It's fine. I'll teach you. We'll try it all until you find all the things you like. I still want you. Don't look so shy," I chuckle.

"I'm a fast learner. If you tell me what I'm supposed to do—"

"I've got you, darlin'," I say against her lips.

I then take them in a passionate kiss as I push a finger inside her. Her moans begin to fill the room, and her pussy becomes more and more wet. I back her toward the bed until impatience kicks in.

Lifting her onto my waist, I continue to devour her mouth as I get us to the bed. I climb on and then begin to kiss my way down her body. I can't stop running my hands over her soft skin.

Even in my impatience I won't rush her pleasure nor mine. I will kiss every inch of her skin if it takes all night and kills me to do so.

"Chance," she cries out as she bucks up off the bed.

I move from kissing her inner thigh while I rub her nub to going in for my first taste. This causes her to lock her legs around my head and lift her upper body onto her shoulders. I'm so turned on; I groan into her core and dive in deeper.

I don't stop for a second. It's too good and I want her too much. Still not able to get enough, I angle my head and push in deeper with my tongue. I feast on her like my favorite snack. She tastes so fucking good.

"Chance, oh my God. I don't know if I can take anymore," she cries.

"I can feel you holding back. You can come, baby. That's what I'm here for. Let me have it."

"Yes, *yeess*," she drags out.

When her body starts to shake. I can do nothing but smile. Her juices fill my mouth as she convulses with pleasure. I reach for her breasts and knead them in my palms. Then I start to lick and suck my way back up her body. When I get to her breasts, I move to take one of her nipples into my mouth.

Jo reaches to claw her nails across my shoulders. Goosebumps raise across her skin as I mirror the gesture against her thigh. She continues to call my name and cry out, making me want her even more.

"Fuck, baby. You're killing me. Did you like that?" I ask after pecking her lips.

"Yes."

"Come here, I want you to sit on my face this time," I say as I roll onto my back.

She climbs onto my face hesitantly at first. I palm her ass as I begin to feast on her again. In pure heaven, I hum with joy as she finds her rhythm and begins to rock her hips.

In no time I have her coming once again. When she falls onto her side to catch her breath, I get up to grab my wallet from my jeans to retrieve a condom. Once I'm suited up, I climb back onto the bed with her.

She sits up and grabs my face to kiss me. I return the kiss, leaning in until she falls back onto the bed as I hover over her. Her thick thighs cradle my sides as my body fits against her soft one.

Hungry for her, I nip and suck at her lips as I take my fill of her sweet mouth and the feel of her warm body beneath mine. All at once it's not enough. I reach to palm the back of her neck as I push my way in.

Breaking the kiss, she buries her face into my neck. I take my time, knowing this is going to hurt. However, Jo locks her legs around me and tugs me in. A yelp leaves her lips as I break through her barrier.

"Fuck," I hiss. "Are you all right, sweetheart?"

She nods her head she still has pressed into my throat. Reaching for her thighs, I begin to rub my hands up and down her skin. This is the most incredible feeling of my life.

"Jo, baby. I need you to tell me you're okay. Use your words, baby. Are you all right?"

"Yes, you're just bigger than … I didn't think I would feel so much or so deep inside me. Can you start to move again?" she says softly sounding as if she's struggling to put her words together.

"Good, girl. It will get better," I murmur and begin to kiss her face as I start to move my hips.

I knew we would be good together. However, I couldn't have dreamed of it being this good. I love that when it becomes pleasurable for her, she begins to move with me.

There is so much passion in our love making. You can hear it in our moans and groans and the way we're panting each other's names. I take my time finding the things she likes and showing her some of what I like.

When she sits on me in reverse cowgirl, she nearly snatches my soul from my body. I may spend the night fucking Jo, but she doesn't just take it. She gives it back and then some.

The one thing I know when we're spent and ready to pass out is that I'm falling completely in love with this girl and I want her to always be mine.

CHAPTER EIGHT

Hang Outs

Chance

Jo's laughter rings out as I elbow her in the side to distract her from playing the video game. She's kicking my ass, and I can be a bit of a sore loser. That and I love hearing that laugh.

"You're still not going to win," she sings.

"Yeah, but you're not about to drop eighty on me either. Where did you learn to play football this well? I mean, you're reading the hell out of my defense and you're making your QB look like a superstar."

"My dad used to play with me all the time and on weekends when he wasn't too busy, we would all watch the games with him. We all picked up the game pretty early.

"JC wanted to play for a while. However, mom couldn't find a league that would accept her and then she found something else to be interested in."

"Oh yeah?"

"Yup, that's when she fell in love with the kitchen. At least I think that was when. *Oh, touchdown*," she croons.

"I have never sucked so much at this game. I want a rematch," I groan.

"Baby, you do know nothing is going to change. I can do this all day," she purrs and gives me that big smile.

"Baby, I like the way that sounds. Hey, have you ever thought about having a game room in your house? I'm not sure if I should add one to the design of my place."

"You absolutely should. Heck yeah, I would want one. You've seen how competitive me and my sisters are. A game room would belong in my home as much as mom's den for book club belongs in hers."

Good to know.

I can't help myself. I have to lean in and take her lips. One minute it's a simple kiss, the next I have her straddling my lap as I kiss her deeply, consuming her mouth.

"Chance, what if Jack comes this way and catches us?"

"I'm not worried about Pop. If he walks in, I'll just introduce him to my girlfriend. No big deal."

"It's a big deal to me. I'm not ready for my mom to find out I'm sleeping with the son of her new boyfriend."

"So you don't want to tell them we're dating?"

She sighs and palms her forehead. "Maybe … I don't know. It's not the boyfriend part. I sort of feel guilty about having sex in mom's house," she whispers the word sex and it's so adorable.

I'm starting to understand Jo more. Coral was right, Jo has been coddled a bit. She's not so much immature, but sometimes she can seem so naïve.

It can be endearing and comical at times. However, it's the sparks of determination that I love most about her. Jo is capable of doing anything she dreams of.

All I want is to be a part of that dream. I knew I wanted her, but that means so much more to me now. We fit together, our night together felt like she became an extension of me.

I cup her pretty face between my hands and look her in the eyes. I'm growing hard with her heat in my lap as images of the other night fill my head.

"Fine, if it will make you feel any better, we'll never have sex under your mother's roof again. However, my name is on the deed here. Daddy, made sure to add me and Hersh once Mama got sick.

"So you can sneak into my bedroom anytime you like, and I'll remind you that you're a grown woman and it's natural for your man to make your body feel good. In fact, I would love a visit from you tonight. I want to be balls deep inside you, baby, as you come all over me," I breathe next to her ear.

"Chance, I'm trying to focus here," she pants.

"So am I. I want to focus on making you come. I don't think I can wait until tonight."

"Ugh, you're impossible." She laughs. "Listen, things are still new. If they ask, we can tell my mom and Jack that we're dating, but I do want to keep the intimate relationship to ourselves. If they don't ask, I don't think we should say anything either."

I chuckle. "As long as you're mine, I don't care. I'll take it."

Before she can say a word or tack on any other stipulations, I take her lips in an all-consuming kiss. She moans into my mouth as I squeeze her breast over her shirt.

"Chance," she breathes as I kiss my way down her neck.

"I want you."

"Your break will be over soon. I thought you were going to take me to the brewery house to show me how it's done."

I stand with her in my arms and head for the back stairs that lead to my room. She wraps her legs around me and buries her face in my neck.

"I am going to show you how it's done. Then we can head to the brewery house. Hersh will be fine without me for a little while."

Her laughter jingles through the air like music. "You're so bad. You know we can't do this all the time, right?"

"Says who? If I can have it my way, this will be my life for as long as I live."

She jerks her head back and searches my face for a few beats. I kick myself for saying too much. I don't want to scare her away. I just got her.

"Chance?"

"Yeah?"

She's silent as her gaze bounces across my face.

"I … I. Nothing."

I peck her lips and smile at her. She has to know how perfect we are for each other. I can see it when I look into her eyes.

Maybe she can see it mine as well. No matter what, I'm going to continue to show her. This can be our forever.

Jo

"See, you're a natural. Pop would be proud," Chance croons in my ear from behind me.

After a few hot rounds of sex, we've finally made it to the brewery house. Chance keeps telling me it's fine, he didn't need to be around, but I get the feeling he's been neglecting work to spend time with me while Hershel has been covering for him.

I roll my eyes. "I didn't do anything but press a few buttons. The machines do all the work."

"Okay, to be fair. We missed today's prep. Mashing and boiling does get a bit more involved. Next time we'll be on time for everything," he chuckles.

"See, I knew it. You're not a very good employee trainer. I might have to report you to a supervisor."

He turns me in his arms to face him and looks down into my eyes. I bite back my smile. Gosh, he's so handsome.

I get goosebumps from the way he looks at me. He runs his strong hands up and down my back and I have no choice other than to melt into him.

"You're my new hire. I am your direct supervisor."

"I don't know about that. I haven't filled out any paperwork so this all could totally be a scam to get into my pants. I think if I had someone else as my supervisor things wouldn't seem so … what's the word I'm looking for?"

"Sketchy," he snorts.

"Yeah, that might be it. Sketchy."

"I'll let Hersh train you this week. And your right, we do need to get you some paperwork, I don't want my girlfriend thinking my family is trying to get free labor out of her."

"You know, I think you just like calling me your girlfriend."

"Yup, I sure do," he says and pecks my lips.

"Well, you can tell my boyfriend I'm not taking a paycheck. I told you I want to help out. I love spending time here."

"Nope, you're getting paid for your time. No arguments."

I reach down and squeeze his growing erection. His eyes widen before they darken with lust. I lick my lips.

"Then I guess we better figure out some other type of compensation because I'm not taking your family's money," I purr.

"Darlin', don't tempt me. I'd love to pay you in orgasms every night."

"Bring it on. I still have so much to learn, don't I?"

"God, you're killing me, Jo."

CHAPTER NINE

This Feels Normal

Jo

"So when are you coming back to the city? We miss you around here," Marty says on the other end of the phone.

He's been chattering away about our friends back home. It all sounds great, and I do miss them, but I've been working on my business plan and brainstorming ideas.

I've been inspired since my first night with Chance. We woke late the next morning and talked about my ideas and plans. He also shared all his plans for the first phase of his growth plan for the B&B.

I love it all for him. Hershel is the oldest, but Chance is the one who wants to take over the place when his father retires. They plan to work the ranch together, but Chance will be the responsible one for it all.

Hershel has always wanted to find his own thing. I guess that's why he became a vet. I've seen him with the horses they have, and he has talked about breeding puppies or taking in rescues.

For the older brother, Hershel is still figuring things out. I think that's why I admire Chance. He makes me see things differently.

For once, I have dared to believe I'm normal and can lead a normal life. The last month has been amazing. I sort of felt guilty about having sex in my mother's house, so Chance has been sneaking me into his room at the B&B when we spend the night together.

I didn't know I would love sex so much. I keep telling myself it's Chance. It wouldn't be the same with anyone else.

"Earth to Jo," Marty croons through the phone, grabbing my attention back to our call.

"Oh, I'm sorry. I miss you guys too. I was thinking about coming in to spend some time with my dad.

"I'll probably stay a week or two. I have a lot I'm working on here though. I'll have to find the time."

"This wouldn't have anything to do with the one you kissed, would it?"

"No, I'm creating a new plan for my life. Spring Valley helps me to stay focused."

"All right. If you say so. I just want you to be careful.

"Make sure you know this guy before you fall in with him. You have plenty of friends here who have your back and will kick his ass if he hurts you.

"You just came out of a bad relationship. I would hate to see you rush into another without taking heed to what happened with the last," he says.

I laugh. "You have nothing to worry about. My goals will come first. Listen, I better go. I have a lot more I want to work on before this place is a madhouse. The sisters are coming in and we're all having a game night."

"That sounds fun."

"It is. It's becoming one of my favorite things. The guys are actually inviting friends this time. Mom and Jack already have plans of their own."

"I'll talk to you soon. Remember, I'm here whenever you need me."

"Thanks, Marty. A girl could only hope to have a hundred friends like you."

He chuckles. "Or one and only one."

Chance comes up behind me and kisses my neck. I crane my head to look up at him and smile. I've been sitting in the barn with my laptop waiting for him to get back from his house.

He hasn't allowed me on site yet. However, I haven't pushed for a reason why. I figured he doesn't want me to get hurt on the construction site.

I frown when I see he looks to be a little annoyed. Chance is always so easy going. I search his eyes and worry fills me.

"Later, Marty," I say and hang up.

"You didn't have to hang up your call. I just needed my arms around you," Chance says and pecks my lips.

I put my phone down and turn to look up at him. He's only wearing a sleeveless white T-shirt, showing off his muscled arms and chiseled body. A body I now know very well.

"What's wrong? Did something happen at the house?"

He rolls his eyes. "Lena has been getting on my nerves lately. She's a great designer but you would think this were her house the way she fusses with me about details I want," he huffs.

"Have you thought about letting her go and using someone else?"

"We go back, and I want to keep the business in Spring Valley. I would hate to fire her and ruin a friendship. I just needed to walk away for today."

"Well, let's get your mind off it. We have time before game night," I say.

"Now, you're talking. Meet me in my room in ten," he croons as he slips his hand under my shirt.

"Chance," I chide. "That's not what I meant. Come sit. I want you to take a look at my plan."

"Fine, but I want you in my bed tonight. I missed your cold little feet last night."

I laugh and roll my eyes at him. He places his forehead against mine as he wraps his arms around me. It's like he sucks me into his orb whenever he's around.

I keep telling myself not to fall for him, but he makes it kind of hard not to. Chance is sweet and attentive. I never have to question if he's listening to me or if he hears me.

My heart aches because I know it's not going to last. Yup, I'm going to ruin this, right when it gets good. JJ will strike again.

She always does.

Lena

When Chance said everyone would be meeting at Willowbrook for a game night, I knew I had to be here. I've been trying to get Chance to come out on a date with me after work, but he keeps making the excuse that he has things to do at the inn.

I don't understand why he hasn't made a move yet. We work so well together, although he's ruining my house. Maybe I should stop arguing with him about it.

After all, everyone knows the Harringtons are loaded and Chance could afford any changes I want to make after we move in. It would just save so much time and money if he would listen to what I want now.

"I'm sorry we haven't been able to get together before this. You're going to love Jo. She's funny and so sweet," Dawn says as she drives us to game night.

"It's so nice of Chance to help her acclimate. This is such a good idea," I reply.

"You know Chance. He makes everyone feel welcome. This should be fun."

We pull up to the Willowbrook house and get out of the car. I can see the rest of our friend group is here already. Music can be heard from in the house and the warm night air makes for a great night to hang out in the backyard.

I'm not surprised when we walk around to the backyard and find everyone hanging out by the firepit. There's such a chill vibe happening. I'm a little surprised to see Mayor Cash here.

He's close to his cousins but I would think he has better things to do than hang with us. He's talking to a curvy Black woman as they hold beers in their hands. Hershel is talking to Lauren who looks like she's on cloud nine and Chance is sitting with a few of our other friends.

I head straight for him. He's sitting in an outdoor armchair as he holds a beer in his hand. I sit on the arm of the chair he's in and take the beer from his hold.

I take a sip and jump right into the conversation. However, I note that Ann and Ginger are glaring at me. I ignore them both. I know they had crushes on Chance in high school. They've always been jealous of our relationship.

"No, I wasn't drinking that, but you go on," Chance says.

I turn to look at him and frown. He looks upset. I laugh it off, knowing he likes to be a private person.

"Is everything okay?" I ask.

"What are you doing?"

"What do you mean? Do you want it back?" I say holding the beer back in his direction.

"No. You keep it and the seat."

With that, he gets up and walks away. I'm left feeling a little confused and embarrassed. Running a hand through my hair, I slide into the seat fully and slump down in it.

Chance

"Baby, I have no idea what that was about. Please look at me, Jo," I plead.

I'm fuming. I don't know what Lena was thinking. I was already pissed when she practically sat on top of me, but I was livid when Jo walked out right as Lena leaned in and took my beer to sip from it like that was a cool thing to do.

I know what it had to look like to Jo, but it's anything but that. I'm so in love with this woman standing before me. I haven't pushed her to tell anyone else what we're doing but she has to know I'm only hers.

I reach for her chin and turn her face to mine. It kills me to see the tears swimming in her eyes as her lips tremble. I peck her soft lips, not able to help myself.

"You know I'm crazy about you, Jo. Lena is just a friend. We've known each other for a long time. She might be a little too familiar as a result, but that has nothing to do with how I feel," I say against her lips.

"You should go back out there with your friends. I need a minute," she says just above a whisper.

"Jo, please. I hate seeing you like this. Talk to me."

"You're not going to like what I say if we talk now," she bites out.

"What do you mean by that?"

"I think we should cool things down. I didn't mean for this to happen. I tried to tell you we would be better as friends. I … you're better off without me."

"No, Jo. I'm not. I'm happier with you. I'm more driven, more focused.

"Look what we accomplished earlier. Think about what we talked about and how things just clicked as we worked together. There are two things I know for sure.

"You belong here in Spring Valley, and you belong here with me. Why can't you see that? Why won't you allow me to show you that? I'm in lo—"

"Don't. Don't you dare say that. Not now. Just give me some space, Chance."

I nod and pull my hand down my face. There is something holding her back and I don't know how to get over or around it. So I back away and rejoin our friends.

CHAPTER TEN

Conflicted Heart

Jo

"Good morning, big head," Mel sings as I walk into the kitchen.

My head is throbbing. I tried my best to enjoy last night, but I never did recover from seeing how Lena felt so comfortable to be all over Chance. This is exactly why I wanted to remain friends.

It's happening.

I sobbed myself to sleep, knowing what's coming for me, for Chance. I don't want to see him hurt, so its best things end now. If things end now, he won't lose anything, I won't lose anyone.

"Come sit down, I made breakfast," JC says.

"Good morning," I mumble to them both.

"We need to talk," Mel says.

"About what? Is Mom okay?"

I take a seat as my heart races. What if it's not Chance who gets hurt this time but me. I would never forgive myself.

"Mom is fine, but we've been talking and we both noticed something," Mel says.

"Oh really, what's that?"

"It's happening again."

"What's happening again?" I look at JC in confusion.

"We're not sure. I mean, we never know what's wrong, but we know when something is wrong."

"Yeah, it happened when we first came to stay with you guys and then again around the time you were in the second grade and again when Mom and Uncle Ralph announced their divorce," JC adds.

"It's like your light starts to go out. You begin to draw into yourself. It happened last night. That got us to talking," Mel continues.

"We like Chance, and we know he's crazy about you."

"More than you can even imagine," Mel scoffs under her breath.

"Chance? What does he have to do with anything? What was that? What are you guys talking about?"

They both laugh. "Girl, please. You know, we think it's cute you two think we don't know y'all fucking," JC snorts.

"He's been knocking the black off that ass. I see the way you been walking all funny when you try to sneak your ass back in this house," Mel says as she rolls her eyes at me.

"Fucking her ass bowlegged," JC sings.

"Who you telling. Have you seen the goofy look on his face when she's around? A blind man could tell he's been bussing that wide open."

"Okay, okay. I've been sleeping with him. What does that have to do with anything?"

"Listen, Jo. I love you, baby girl. You're more than my cousin. You're my baby sister."

"Our baby sister. I thought you were mad that we had to come live with you at first. Maybe that was the reason for the change, but then it happened again and again," JC says.

"Oh my God, JC. You two are everything to me. I look up to both of you. I was so happy when Mom brought you guys home," I say as I begin to sob.

"Hey, hey, Jo-Jo. We just want you to talk to us. Chance is the first guy we've seen you truly interested in. Not dating to people please but you genuinely like him," Mel coos.

"I … I. I'm a jinx. Jo the Jinx. I was never mad at Mom for bringing you guys home.

"I was sad because I ruined your lives. Whenever people I love are happy and they spend too much time around me, I ruin their lives. I break up love," I sob.

"What?" Mel and JC gasp in unison.

"You guys were so happy. Your dad was around, and your mom wasn't sick. Then I started coming over for sleepovers all the time and … your mom got sick, and your parents started to argue every time I came over.

"Then your mom got better, and things were looking better. You two were excited about that trip to Disney your dad was going to take you on. So excited, JC asked my mom could I go. Uncle Kurt said I could, but your mom died, and he never came back or took us to Disney.

"I took everything from you. You were so sad and heartbroken, and it was all my fault. I jinxed everything," I sob.

"See, I told you they dropped her little ass on her head before we moved in. I bet Uncle Ralph did it. His ass do be clumsy sometimes," JC says.

"Shut up, Jodie Cadence Simpson-Marks," Mel snaps, she then coos to me. "Baby girl, even if all those things lined up to be true, how would that make any of it your fault?"

I swipe at my tears. "In second grade, there was a reason I was so sad. Remember Nancy?"

"The little buck tooth girl you used to hang with?" Mel asks.

"Yeah," I snort.

"Didn't she move away or something?"

"Yeah. We spent so much time together that summer. I was always at her house, or her mom would take us to work with her. Then one day while we were playing at her house her dad come home.

"Her parents started fighting and two weeks later they moved. Nancy wrote me a few letters after, but her dad was gone, and she didn't seem happy like she was before they left," I explain.

"Again, not your fault."

"Lord knows you better not try to say Mom and Uncle Ralph's divorce had anything to do with you," JC says.

"Well, they did begin to start arguing a lot after I came back from college. I moved out into my own place, hoping I wouldn't jinx it all," I murmur.

"Jodie Ann Marks. You're no more a jinx than I'm a rich white cowgirl, married to a professional football superstar," Mel chides. "Shit happens. Our mom had been sick for a long time and wouldn't tell anyone.

"She and Daddy fought all the time. Those arguments had nothing to do with you. And he never took us to Disney because he was a selfish liar."

"I'm still trying to understand what you think you're jinxing now?" JC says.

"Chance has so much going for him. If he keeps dating me, it could all be ruined. I jinx love and happiness. I think last night was for the best."

"What happened last night?"

"We broke up," I mutter.

"Ha, so you think," JC laughs hysterically.

"What are you talking about now?"

"That man slept on the couch. He didn't leave this house last night. He's waiting to—"

"Jo, can we talk?"

I startle and turn to find Chance staring at me. I had no idea he was here. My heart sinks. How much did he hear?

"Talk to the man. You're not a jinx, sis. Some really bad things happened around you as a little girl and you've carried that into adulthood.

"Like Mom would say, don't let your past rob you of your future. We're all a work in progress, but you have to be willing to take the steps to progress," Mel whispers in my ear as she hugs me tight.

I nod as she releases me. Then I get up to walk over to Chance. He pulls me into a tight hug when I reach him and kisses the top of my head.

"You could never be a jinx in my life. I love you, Jo. I want to do life with you.

"Those things weren't your fault. You were a little girl surrounded by life. All of that was as much your fault as my mama's death was mine.

"I get it. For a while, I did blame myself. Then you showed up and brought the light back with you.

"I know you're not a jinx because you're my good luck charm. If you let me, I'll show you we belong together."

"Are you really willing to take that risk with me?"

'Yes, Jo. I am. Like I said, I love you."

"Yeah, I heard you the first time. Chance?"

"Yeah, baby?"

"I don't know if I can say it yet. If I do and you guys are wrong ..."

"I get it. You don't have to say it yet. We'll heal what's broken first and you can say it when you're ready."

My heart swells and the words rest on the tip of my tongue, but I still can't say them.

Mel

"You know that shit is our fault, right?" I say as I glare at JC.

She sighs. "We were little kids. Everyone used to say it."

"Yeah, but we were little assholes about it. Jo the Jinx, JJ? She would cry every time we called her that."

JC widens her eyes at me. "Oh boy. I'll pay for her to talk to my therapist. Like I was supposed to know calling a six-year-old a jinx because I lost Candyland was going to scar her for life."

"Therapist? What therapist?"

"The one I'm seeing to get my shit together." She rolls her eyes.

"Jo has moved here permanently. I don't think she's going to drive five to six hours to go see ..."

I trial off and narrow my eyes. Things begin to click into place. I've been so busy running Cash and Thomas's offices, I haven't had time to dig into all the questions I've had for my little sister.

Well, I'm about to get into that ass now. I fold my arms over my chest. Then lean in and hiss at her.

"How long have you been living here and where the fuck do you stay while you lie to Mom about it?"

"It's not like that. Besides, we're talking about Jo, not me."

"Then let's talk about you, Jodie. What's going on?"

"It was easier to live here when the office assigned the project to me. I needed to get away and start to move forward. You know Mom.

"She sees everything. I couldn't move in here. I got a place in Kelly. It's close enough and no one knows me there except …"

"Oh my God. He knows. Now so much makes sense."

"Mel, I know that look. It's not what you think. Things are complicated and I'm doing my best to breathe.

"None of this has anything to do with you guys. I was blindsided and he was there and … I'm sorry."

"Don't apologize to me. That's going to be a you and Mom thing if he gets hurt but that's not my concern. You, Jodie Cadence, are. Tell me how I can help."

Chance

"Everything all right, bro?" Hershel asks as I stand staring into space as I man the grill for lunch service.

I turn to him and focus. He has a look of concern in his eyes. I give him a nod.

"Yeah, I'm all right. A lot on my mind."

I can't get my mind off what I overheard Jo say to JC and Mel. I can't imagine how she must have felt as a small girl. To carry those feelings all this time.

I took a few psych and sociology classes on the side while getting my business degree. I know trauma can be different for children. From what Jo has told me she was about five or six when her cousins lost their mom and came to leave with her.

I'm hurting for her because she thinks she's the cause of so much that had nothing to do with her. Then there is Lena. I'm going to need to let her go.

I don't like what she did last night. The more I think about it the more it pisses me off. I don't know what the fuck she was thinking, but I don't feel comfortable working with her now.

"Thinking about Jo or Lena?"

"You picked up on that too?"

"Lena has never gotten over you. I was surprised when I heard you hired her. I thought you would have seen the potential problem there."

"Come on, man. That was in junior high school. We dated for what? Six months max. Besides, she broke up with me."

"Yeah, cause Mama threatened her."

"What?"

He scoffs. "Mama caught Lena and her friends buying condoms and talking about putting holes in them to trap their boyfriends. They made a pregnancy pact and Mama heard it all.

"She went to Lena's house to talk to her and her mama. She told Lena to stay away from you and told her mama she'd ruin their family if Lena did indeed try to trap you," he explains.

"How do you know all this?"

"You were at basketball camp. I broke my arm, remember? I was home for the summer and was there for it all.

"Lena told me how sorry she was and that she felt stupid for going along with her friends. She also asked me not to say anything. Once you guys broke up and you moved on with Penny Morris, I didn't see a point in telling you."

"Mom was something else. I miss her."

"Yeah, me too. She would have loved Jo."

"I know."

CHAPTER ELEVEN

Back Off

Chance

"Hey, I thought you were giving everyone the day off today," Lena says as she walks into the house where I'm waiting for her.

"I did. I asked you here so we could talk," I reply.

Her eyes light up and she looks all fluttered as she begins to fidget and fluff at her hair. How the fuck did I miss this before? I stifle a groan as it all becomes clear.

"Listen, I think somehow you got the wrong idea about us. I'm building this house for my girlfriend. I hired you to help me do this for her."

"You said you didn't have a girlfriend yet. That … Oh my God." She palms her face. "Jo. You're building this place for Jo. Chance, I … I. I'm such an idiot.

"I thought you … We had this great connection when we dated. I assumed. Shit, I thought Jo was just new around here and you were being nice to her because your dad is dating her mom.

"I didn't know you guys were … She's been coming here for months. Shit. Never mind."

"This isn't going to be a problem, is it?" I say as she stammers all over herself.

"No. Um. Actually, I have a friend who I can refer you to. I've done most of the work already.

"Maybe she can take over for me. I'm so embarrassed. Jo is lovely. Dawn told me I would love her, and she was right."

She pushes a hand through the front of her hair, and her cheeks turn red. I haven't figured out how I feel about any of this yet. I do know that I woke up, and my first mind said she has to go.

"Fuck, does everyone else know you two are dating?"

"We've never officially announced our relationship, but I think others have figured it out. Ginger and Beck know for sure," I reply.

"I'm so sorry, Chance. I misread this entire situation so badly."

"I probably should have done things differently. I do thank you for all your help."

"I wish you all the best. I hope I get to come to a game night when the house is done so I can see the final results. You're a good one, Chance. See you around," Lena says as she comes to give me a hug.

I embrace her quickly and then take a step back. She looks crestfallen as she nods and turns to leave. I sigh and shake my head.

I thought she was going to take that harder. Once she's gone, I turn in a circle as I look around the place. This is happening.

I'm building Jo a house. This will show her she's no jinx and she belongs with me. I can't wait to show her.

Jo

"If you're not going to come back to the city, maybe I can come there to hang with you. You make this place sound like it's some type of magic," Marty says into the phone.

"It is. Spring Valley is … it's … ugh. I can't find the words. It's like a plate of soul food. It has comfort and warmth and it makes everything feel better," I gush.

"Is it the place or is something else holding you there?"

"What do you mean?"

"What happened with that guy? Are you seeing him?"

"I'm happy. That's all that matters."

"You were happy while you were dating Jarold too. Look at how that turned out."

I sigh and roll my eyes. I've been in such a good mood today. Mel, JC, and I spent some time together and did some more talking.

I'm even thinking about going to see the therapist JC recommended. They're right. I can't blame myself anymore.

I'm starting to believe this is my next step forward. Letting go of the past. I won't know if I don't try.

"Thanks for your concern, Marty. I appreciate it, I do."

"But you're not going to listen to me until he proves me right. You've known this guy for how long? You can't trust him, Jo. Not like—"

"I'll talk to you later, Marty. Tell Stephanie I said hi."

I hang up before he can reply. There was a time I thought he was batting for the same team. I have no problem with that.

Heck, if he would date anyone, that would get him out of my business. About a month ago he told me he's been seeing some girl named Stephanie.

Hopefully, he'll call her and be in her business. I love my friend, but I'm tired of him telling me the same thing. Chance isn't Jarold and I'm not going to treat him like he is.

CHAPTER TWELVE

Perfect Together

Chance

"Watch your step, we're almost there," I say into Jo's ear.

"What are you up to?" She laughs. "Shouldn't we be turning those rooms."

"Hersh is doing that for me. I want to show you something. Now stop asking questions."

"But all my questions are how I figured out how to make you come so hard last night. Do you really want me to stop?"

I snort and lean in to dip my head and bite her ear. Last night was amazing. I never had a partner question in such detail how to pleasure me.

Jo took my answers and doubled down on them. I thought my head was going to explode. Shit, my cock did.

"Keep it up and I'm going to bend you over and return the favor," I say into her ear.

"Talk is cheap, Harrington. I need to see some action." She giggles as I bring us to a stop and nuzzle her neck.

I release the blindfold from her eyes and wait. I don't realize I'm holding my breath until Jo pops her hip to the side and turns to look over her shoulder at me.

"You guys are building a second barn? But why?"

I chuckle. "It's not a barn. We just haven't finished building the place out."

"What is it for?"

"The spa. Pop loves the idea."

"Are you serious? You're building a spa? I thought you were joking around."

"No. I meant it. I thought you could interview for the management position or as one of the therapists," I say as I search her gaze.

She snorts. "I hope your dad is the one interviewing. I'm sort of sleeping with you, so I don't think I'm going to get an objective interview at all."

"You're already hired. I'm using your design ideas to finish the place."

"I can't believe you're doing this. What about when I leave to start my business? What if—"

I place my finger over her lips. I already see the future we want. They don't have to be separate things. I know what she's about to say.

"We belong together. I'm not going anywhere and you're going to be right here with me. Now, come on. We should head back for that conference call for the family reunion that's looking to book with us."

"Look at you. Multitasking and building your version of your empire."

I give her a wink. "I can't do it without my partner in crime. Come on, baby. Our empire calls."

Jo

It's been a long day. My face hurts from all the smiling I've done. Chance is adding a spa to the ranch. A spa where I can work and live here.

I know I said I wanted to do my own thing, but this feels so right. The more I work here with Chance, the more it feels like this is where my life belongs.

For the last month, I've been helping at the B&B and brewery. It's a lot of work, but I like it. Once the spa is up and running, I know I'm going to love it here.

Days filled with working with Chance and our family and nights like this. We're in Chance's room lying on his bed. Music is playing and we're staring into each other's eyes.

He reaches to brush a lock of hair out of my face. I smile and cover his hand with mine. He returns the smile and leans in to peck my lips.

"What are you thinking about?" he asks.

"I'm happy. Things are starting to feel like they make sense," I reply.

"We make a great team. I couldn't have gotten so much done today without you," he murmurs.

"Who would have thought my mom's job interview would have led to all of this?"

"I'm so glad she came for that interview. Look at all the good that's come to Spring Valley since. Good thing I found you first and not Hersh," he chuckles.

"What's that supposed to mean?"

"You really didn't know me and my brother had a thing for you?"

I gasp. "No. What are you talking about?"

He laughs and shakes his head. "Nothing. Nothing at all."

"We should probably get up and shower. It's been a long day," I say and bite my lip.

"As long as you shower with me. I think you need my help washing your back and I definitely have a few other things I want to help you soap up."

"You're so nasty," I laugh.

"You haven't seen nasty yet. Come on before I pounce on you right here."

"You're so bossy," I tease.

He gets up and lifts me from the bed, tossing me over his shoulder. I yelp and begin to laugh as he heads for his bathroom. Chance palms my butt and gives it a squeeze.

I then feel him nuzzle my shirt away from my torso before his soft lips dance across my skin. Suddenly, he stops in the middle bathroom and places me on my feet. As I look up at him, I can't remember why I was so adamant about not dating him.

I dare to think that I have been wrong. I can have a happily ever after. As if reading my mind, he cups the side of my face and captures my lips.

"You can breathe, Jo. This is our forever. You're my forever. We work and nothing can tear us apart. I love you," he breathes against my lips.

He kisses me again, scrambling my thoughts. Lifting onto my toes, I then lock my fingers in his hair and hold him to me. We begin to work on each other's clothes as he makes love to my mouth.

However, the buzzer in his room that serves as the buzzer for the front desk goes off. I whimper as he pulls away. I know he can't ignore it.

It's his night to be on duty. He groans and kisses my forehead. His blue eyes are filled with longing as he looks back at me.

"Go ahead and shower. I'll be back as soon as I can," he says.

I nod and watch him go. I would go down with him, but mom is here tonight.

I should have gone back to Willowbrook after work was over. I still haven't mentioned to my mom that I spend the night here with Chance at least a few times a week. I know it's a conversation we should have soon.

***

"Oh my God, Jo. Fuck, baby," Chance groans as I go down on him.

I fell asleep before he got back from whatever called him away. I had been waiting for him naked, hoping he would get the point.

However, when I woke to use the bathroom in the middle of the night, I found him asleep next to me.

"Yes, baby. I love that mouth. Suck it harder. Take me deeper.

"Yes, that's a good girl. You know just what I like, baby. You were made for me," he groans.

I smile and hum around him. I've only gone down on him a few times, but he seems to love every time I do. I shift to get on my knees between his legs and put my hands to work as I suck harder while stroking him.

Saliva drips down my hands as he grows increasingly hard. Now that I know he's fully awake, I want to feel him inside of me. I climb his body and lean in to kiss his lips.

He reaches for a condom from his side table and breaks the kiss to bite into. I sit up to allow him to roll it on. I watch as he places the rubber over his thick length.

"Like what you see, baby?"

"Yup, let me show you how much," I say with a smile.

He sits up and presses his nose to mine. I smile and press my lips to his. The events of the day begin to play in my head.

How can I not fall for him? Chance gets me and he's showing me that with each day. I put more into the kiss as he devours me.

He takes over the kiss and flips me onto my back. His breath is still minty from brushing his teeth before bed which tells me he hasn't been sleeping that long. I turn to glance at the clock and just like that he thrusts into my already wet core.

I lock my legs around his waist as he reaches for my hands and laces our fingers together. I don't know why I'm so surprised by his slow pace. He's dragging his thick dick back and forth through my walls with slow, long, deep strokes.

All while staring me deep in the eyes. I'd be lying if I said the connection didn't feel different from all the other times we've ever had sex. There's no doubt he's making love to me.

"Chance," I cry out as he starts to hit my spot repeatedly.

He groans and dips his head to take one of my nipples into his mouth. My walls tighten around him. I begin to come as I call his name louder.

"Jo, baby. You feel so good, but you're kind of loud, baby. I turned the music off before I got in bed. Someone might hear you," he grunts into my ear.

My mind glitches. I know his words are important and I should focus on them, but I can't. Not when he's making love to me like this.

He hasn't stopped thrusting, and I can't stop coming. Chance has mastered making my body his. He knows just how to trigger me and to leave me a mess, he can hold in the palm of his hand.

He's so hard and deep. Yet there's something so sweet and gentle about it. I cry out again, causing him to chuckle sexily and capture my lips.

He keeps rolling his hips into me. When he picks up the pace and begins to swell inside me, I can't help moaning loudly in his mouth.

"Fuck, Jo. I love you so much. I'll never get enough of you." He tightens his hands against mine as we lock eyes.

"Chance, oh my God. I … you … I … I'm coming. You feel amazing. I'm coming so hard."

"I feel you, baby. Come for me. Show me how much you love me. I know you do. Come for me and show me what you can't say."

My toes curl and I begin to shake beneath him. I come so hard I see stars. He's right. I can't say it yet, but my body doesn't know how to hide it.

CHAPTER THIRTEEN

Lake Magic

Jo

"A picnic? This is so sweet, Chance. I didn't know this lake was here," I say as Chance spreads a blanket for us to sit on.

There is so much land on this ranch, I still don't believe I've seen it all. The way Chance talks of expansion and all the structures we can add and still have land left for the next three or four generations to make their mark, I'm sure there's plenty I still have to learn about this place. Yes, we talk of the future here.

I'm getting used to all the talk of our future and the growth of his family's legacy. Jack treats me so much like his daughter and has welcomed me into their business so easily it's kind of hard not to get caught up in it all.

"This was my mother's favorite spot. She loved it here. I can remember all the times she would bring me and Hersh out here to play," he says wistfully.

"I wish I could have met her."

"I wish she would have met you too. I think she would have loved you. To be honest, she would have loved your entire family. I'm sure she and your mom would have been best friends."

"That would have been interesting," I chuckle.

"Yeah, it would have. I wouldn't have to sneak you into my bedroom because you're still worried about your mom and my dad dating. I'd be able to share with the world that I'm dating the most wonderful woman in the world," he croons as he helps me to sit and then claims the seat behind me, cradling me in between his legs.

"I don't know about all that. I'm still a work in progress. Besides, I was thinking about sitting down with mom soon. My therapist thinks it's best if I do."

Chance kisses the top of my head. "I'm so proud of you. You say work in progress, I say amazing. I'm watching you do the work.

"You're happier. You express your feelings easier. I adore you for who you are and who you're becoming," he says thoughtfully.

"Thanks. That means a lot to me. Do you want to be there when I talk to Mom and Jack?"

"Of course, if you want me there, I'm there. Are you hungry? I made the same basket my mom always made us."

"Oh, yeah? Sure, I could eat. Sounds like there's a good story behind that. Are you going to share?"

He chuckles and kisses my neck. "Yeah, there is a story. I was sort of a brat. I went through this stage where I wouldn't eat but three things. Chicken nuggets and fries, peanut butter and jelly, and hot dogs.

"Hersh was so sick of PB&J sandwiches. We started fighting about what lunch mom would bring for our picnics, so mom started to make grilled cheese sandwiches. That first time I didn't want them.

"Mom sat here patient as ever and told me those grilled cheese sandwiches were special. They were what made this place magic and as long as we made them and ate them here, the lake would grant us a wish whenever we had them here together as a family," he explains.

"That's such a sweet story. Did your wishes ever come true?"

"All the time. Mom and Pop would ask us what we wished for, and they would make it come true. Every wish I've ever made here but one has come true," he says regretfully.

"Can I ask what that wish was?"

"I wished for mom to get better. I sat here as a grown man and made that wish as I ate enough grilled cheese sandwiches to make myself sick. That's why I understood how you could still believe a belief from your childhood could still hold so much power."

"And you still want to eat them now?"

"Yes, I believe that there are some things that remain special even when they aren't what we think they are. This lake does have magic. It might not work the way I thought it did, but it's still special."

"What makes you say that?"

"Because my family has laughed and smiled the most when we were right here. This is where Harrington magic lives. The last time Mama was able to come out here and sit with me, she had this smile on her face that I'll never forget.

"That smile will forever be a reminder that she lived, loved, and laughed on her terms. I think she was tired and ready to let go. We didn't want her to, but she was ready. I believe as long as we are ready, we can move forward in life no matter what."

"Are you ready, Chance?"

"Yes, Jo. I'm ready and waiting for my other half to be ready with me."

I crane my head to look up into his eyes. He searches my face with his gaze. Reaching for my face, he cups it and runs his thumb across my lips.

"What exactly are you ready for?"

"Everything and anything that comes our way. I want you, Jo. I want the life we've been planning. We may not say it's our life.

"At least, you're not ready to admit it's ours, but it's ours. All the talks have painted a picture of us for me. It's like my mama used to say.

"It's not yours until you claim it in your heart and hold on tight. I'm claiming you in my heart, Jo. I'm holding on as tight as I can," he says.

"I love you," I blurt out.

He presses his forehead to mine. Then he releases a breathy chuckle. Capturing my lips in a deep kiss, he devours my mouth thoroughly.

"I know, but it feels damn good to hear you say it. I love you too, Jodie. I love you more than you could probably know."

Courtland

"I still think this is a bad idea. You don't know my brother-in-law. He's not going to roll over and take this. Allow me—"

"Allow you to what? Fail again. You have been given opportunity after opportunity to get this done. Now it's my turn to step in."

I sigh and drag a hand down my face. This is what I get. First Betty-Lou, now this.

This is a dumb plan and it's going to backfire. If it doesn't it's still going to cause trouble for me. I don't like it, but I haven't figured out how to tell the mob no and still keep my head.

I'll just have to hold my breath while they try Jack and hope he sticks to the stubborn streak that works in his favor all the time. Jack isn't stupid. Neither is my son.

"I'm telling you if you allow me to try one more time, we're better off. I know Harrington."

"You know a lot but none of your knowledge has gotten my employers what they want. You can either help me or get out of my way. If you chose to remain in my way, you're not going to like the results."

"Fine," I bite out.

Fuck.

Chance

I'm still on cloud nine after my date with Jo. Hearing her say she loves me was a gift in itself. I've fallen so hard for her.

The house has been going to plan. It will be done right on time for Thanksgiving. I'm thinking about proposing before I give her the house or right after the New Year.

I smile as I scroll through a site looking at engagement rings. I'm hoping to get an idea of what I plan to get for her. I want a ring that says it all.

"Good evening."

I look up from my phone. I've been so focused on rings, I hadn't heard anyone walk in. There's a man standing at the desk smiling back at me.

I don't get a settling feeling from his presence. I push that thought aside and put my phone down. No matter what, we always give great customer service.

"Good evening. Do you have a reservation with us?"

"No, I don't. I was hoping you had a room available. I'm passing through and hoped I'd have some luck."

"Just you?"

"Yes. Been that way for a few years now," he says and gives a chuckle.

"Looks like you're in luck. We have one room left. It's one of the smaller rooms, but it has a great view of the ranch."

"That will be great."

"How long will you be with us?"

"You can book me for the next week for now if that's possible," he says with a wolfish smile.

I knit my brows. He said he was passing through. Those just passing through stay for a night or two. Not a week.

However, I keep my thoughts to myself and ask for his ID and credit card. He hands over his information. I take a mental note of his address and name.

He's not from around here. I pretty much already knew that. I've never seen him before.

"Okay, here's your key. I just need your signature here and you're all set."

"Can you tell me what time the brewery opens?" he asks as he signs.

"Sure, breakfast starts at eight. The brewery opens at one, but we offer lunch around noon. You can usually order a beer around then off the taps."

"Sounds good. You guys have a solid business going here. I can't wait to see more of the brewery."

"That we do. It's a family business. Here's your card and ID, Mr. Peterson. Welcome to Harringtons and please enjoy your stay. Let us know if we can help you with anything."

"I sure will. See you soon, young man."

I purse my lips as I watch him go. That feeling still sitting in the pit of my belly. I try to shrug it off and get back to work.

However, twenty minutes later I'm still trying to figure out what it is about that guy that rubbed me wrong. It isn't until Jo appears through the side entrance and waves before she sneaks up to me room, that I let it go for the night.

CHAPTER FOURTEEN

Things Shake Up

Jo

"Hey, Jo. Wendy is looking for you. Something about the spa," Lauren says as she comes to the front desk.

I've been manning the phones and going through the website bookings to make sure there are no overlaps. It doesn't happen often, but Hershel and Chance said there is a glitch every now and then with the system.

I'm also waiting for an appointment for a bridal shower. I'm going to show them around and get the planning for their event started. The word has gotten out and everyone who's anyone wants to throw an event here now.

I'm so proud of Chance. Jack has been happy as well. Quite a few of the events have brought in more B&B business.

"Have you seen Chance or Hershel? Someone will need to take over," I say.

"I can do it. Lunch is slow. They have more than enough help back there," she says.

I nod and get up. Lauren used to help out at the desk all the time. I know she's capable.

I head out to the new spa structure, looking for Wendy. She's the interior designer for the new addition. I haven't asked Chance why he's not using Lena.

From what I've heard, he let her go from his house project. I can't help but wonder if that was because of us. I see her in town sometimes and she's been cordial.

I don't know her enough to have any opinions about her. She hasn't been to any of the events I've been to that Chance's other friends have attended. I haven't given too much thought to that because plenty of his friends have been too busy to link up.

"Oh, great. You're here. The wallpaper we ordered was discontinued. I'm still trying to track it down elsewhere to see if I can get enough but chances are we're going to need to choose something else.

"Here, look through these. They have the same vibe but vary a bit from the original design. Let me know what you think," Wendy rattles off as soon as she sees me.

"Where's Chance? Shouldn't this be his final say?"

"He's at the house. He told me to talk to you. He also wants you to greenlight which lights we're going to go with."

"Really?"

"Yup. Don't sound so surprised. He's obsessed with you. Haven't you noticed how much he leans on your opinion?"

"No, not really."

"You guys are the perfect power couple. I can't wait to make my standing appointments for my spa days. This place looks awesome already," she gushes.

My heart swells. With each day I can see my life here with Chance more and more. This all feels like home to me.

Wendy is right. The place is starting to look amazing. Chance believes we'll be able to do a grand opening within the next month or so.

Bell has already promised to come. Chance and I will be interviewing new hires together, making this all real.

"I'm excited too. Let's go with this one and for the lights. I love the chrome ones with the swirly design."

"Oh, I love those. They remind me of flames or something. I love that they have multiple settings and dimmers. Good choice. Chance is right to trust you," she says.

"Anything else? I want to get back so Lauren can get back to her post."

"Nope, all good. Thanks."

I nod and turn to head back. When I walk out of the spa building, I run right into Mr. Peterson. He's one of the guests at the inn.

He's been here for about three weeks, much to Chance's annoyance. Something about this man rubs him the wrong way. I have to admit; he is a little shifty if you ask me.

"Ah, sorry about that. I've been so curious about this structure. I thought I'd try to get a peek.

"Rumor in town says it's going to be a spa. I was a little surprised by that. I was under the impression the Harringtons know the B&B and beer industries. Isn't a spa a bit risky?"

"No, it's not. They have a professional consulting them," I bite out.

"I meant no harm. I'd just hate to see them devalue such a great business model."

"Mr. Peterson. I don't know how that's any of your business as a guest. My boyfriend and his family have run this place for years. They know what it takes to keep it running. I'm sure they'll be just fine," I snap.

"Yes. I guess you are right. Although, when the place is mine, I don't think this will be in line with how I plan to run the place."

"Excuse me?" I hiss as my heart begins to race.

"I probably shouldn't be saying this, but my attorney will be here in the morning with the petitions. This land belongs to me, and I plan to take it back."

My heart sinks into my stomach as I stand with my mouth hanging open. I have to be hearing things. Suddenly, my dreams are all crumbling in front of my eyes.

Not just my dreams, but Chance's as well. It's happening. I was right.

How could I have done this to Chance? I think I'm going to be sick. I'm a jinx.

Everything is falling apart.

Chance

I knew I didn't like that son of a bitch. He's been lurking around for weeks. I almost put my fist through a wall when Jo told us what that bastard said to her.

How the fuck does he think he has a claim on our land? Pop has no idea who he is, and Hershel and I have never seen him before he showed up here. Things were going so well, now this.

It's like I can feel Jo pulling away from me. I started to notice it after Cash and Pop were able to calm me down. At first, I thought she was surprised by my temper.

Now, I see it has nothing to do with my temper at all. I groan internally as I think of what this could be about. She was making such progress but as my mind taunts me about making a wish at the lake a month ago during our date, I know I'm not wrong.

Old habits die hard. I'm not about to lose Jo or my family's land. I will fight until the death if I have to. This is our home and always has been.

"Now that we're all here and we're thinking with clearer heads, let's come up with a plan of action. Jack, you know for sure this land has always been in your family's name. There has never been some type of deed exchange for parcels or anything?"

"No, we've never needed to sell off anything. Not a single acre," Pop says.

"He's right. I've been in the archives at the library reading about the town's history. There were three founding families. Only two remain. The Harringtons are one of them. There are maps and dated surveys for the land. It's all documented," Miss Coral says.

"Surveys that line up with the fence lines to a Tee. I have copies of everything. I keep it all in the safe," Pop says.

"For now, we don't know what his lawyer has planned. We'll have to wait until he files in the morning, but you gather everything you have and get copies ready. I'll call Uncle Ralph.

"Something stinks and I don't like it. First all the BS with Cash now this. This isn't a coincidence, I bet my left ass cheek on that," Mel says.

"You girls have done nothing but fix our messes since you arrived here. I want to thank you all," Pop says.

"Y'all folks are kind of messy," Mel taunts and snickers. "But I've handled worse. You guys' drama feels more like a vacation if you ask me."

"I'm going to need a vacation," Cash grumbles.

"Don't joke like that. Mel will have one booked for you and Emma in less than twenty-four hours," JC says.

"Who's joking. I could use a day or week away from all of this. If only I had the time, I would get out of here," Cash says.

I look to Mel, and she has pulled out her phone. From the determined look on her face, I get the feeling JC might be right. With everything going on, I wouldn't blame Cash for taking off for a bit.

"Well, there's nothing else we can do tonight, and I have an early morning so I'm calling it," JC says as she stands and yawns.

CHAPTER FIFTEEN

Trying to Kickback

Jo

"You do know I'm not going to allow them to take anything from Jack or Cash, don't you?" Mel whispers into my ear.

I turn to look at her and see the concern in her eyes. "I know," I murmur.

"Then why the long face?"

I shrug, not wanting to talk about my feelings. We're at Luke's for drinks and axe throwing with Hershel, Chance, and their friends. We're supposed to be blowing off steam, but I've been lost in my head.

I've been sick to my stomach all week. Mel and Dad have been telling everyone not to worry, but I can't shake the feeling that all of this is because of me. If Chance and I weren't together, this wouldn't be happening to his family.

Since my run in with Mr. Peterson, Jack has been served with a lawsuit claiming the ranch belongs to Peterson. The progress on the spa has come to a standstill right at the end when we should be planning for the grand opening. Everything has been pushed back.

I stopped going to work at the inn and brewery because I feel like all of this is my fault. I tried to pull away from Chance, but he hasn't made that easy. When I called out of work claiming to be sick, Chance dropped everything to show up at Willowbrook with soup.

He spent the whole day taking care of me. I felt so bad, but I couldn't tell him I lied. The next day, I told him it was that time of month and that's why I had been feeling so crummy the day before.

He gave me the space I asked for for the rest of the week. Now, I'm here at Luke's surrounded by all Chance's friends as I occasionally try to force a smile on my face. Chance has been drinking but he's also been watching me.

"Come dance with me. That will cheer you up," Mel sings.

I glance around for JC in hopes of an escape but she's with Hershel throwing axes. For once she has a genuine smile on her face. I refuse to get in the way of that smile being present.

When I spot Lena throwing back beers with Beck and Dustin, I decide the dance floor might be my best options. My emotions are all over the place.

I get up with Mel and head to the dance floor with her. It's like as soon as we get out there the music changes from an upbeat tone to a slow one. Chance likes to play this one.

"Bad as I Do" by Jacob Hackworth plays while my silly cousin takes the lead. I can't help but smile. I know that's her point.

However, after she spins me one more time, my back is engulfed in heat and the scent of Chance's cologne mixed with beer hits me hard. He gathers my hair in one hand to move it out of the way and dips his head to kiss my neck. Mel smiles at me and nods. I close my eyes and nod back.

"I'm not going to allow you to do this. I love you too much. None of what's going on is your fault.

"You're mine, Jo and I miss you like crazy. You can't keep pushing me away. I belong with you," he says into my ear as he sways with me in his arms.

"But—"

"No, Jo. You're not a jinx. If I have to say that every minute of every day, I'm gonna do it. You're my world. I breathe to be near you."

"Chance, I—"

He spins me until I'm facing him. I open my eyes and our gazes lock. Before I can say a word, he grasps the back of my head and crushes his lips to mine.

I wrap my arms around his neck and lift on my toes as he devours me like he's about to lose me. I melt into him needing him more than I'm willing to admit.

"I don't want to hurt you, but I also don't want to lose you," I whisper.

"I'm right here, Jodie. It's you and me. No matter what."

"Okay, it's not my fault. I'm not a jinx. I don't ruin love," I repeat the words my therapist told me to say when the feeling of being a jinx overwhelms me.

"No, baby. You're not. You're the love of my life. You're my everything, Jodie Ann."

I look into his eyes and see the sincerity of his words. So much weight lifts as I push the doubt away. I won't let this beat me.

"Come for a walk with me, baby."

I nod and take his hand. He walks right by everyone we're here with and leads me outside. Once we're at his truck on the far side of the lot where the light is dimmest, he backs me against the passenger's side door and palms my face to kiss me.

I gasp and release a moan as he moves his lips to my neck as he gropes one of my breasts. Lifting my gaze to the sky, I stand and take all he's giving. It's been a week since we've slept together.

"Chance," I whimper as he slips his hand into my panties after bunching up my dress.

It's warm for a late October night. Even if it weren't I don't know that I would notice as he sets my body on fire. He takes my lips again as he pumps two fingers in and out of me.

"I want you," he groans into my ear.

"What? Here? Now?"

"Yes, I need you, Jo. I've been feeling like I'm losing you. I need to be inside you.

"I need to know I can still call you mine. I want your thick thighs wrapped around my waist while I fuck you 'til you come," he breathes.

"Okay." I nod and lick my lips.

I reach for the waist of my panties and start to push them down. I barely get to step out of them before he has his pants down his hips just before he lifts me onto his waist and thrusts into me.

I close my eyes and hold on tight as he fucks me up against his truck. Chance groans and pants in between kissing the side of my head and face. He's so hard and I'm so wet.

"Fuck, Jo. Baby, you're so amazing. You fit me perfectly.

"I can't lose you, baby. No one is meant for me like you are. Fuck, that's my girl. Keep getting wet for me," he growls.

He reaches for one of my breasts to squeeze it and I begin to convulse against him as he hits my spot over and over. As if that's not enough, he releases my breast and reaches to grab a handful of my hair.

It surprises me at first, but once he forces my eyes on him as he looks me deeply in the eyes, I can't help but come for him again. I bite my lip as I stare back at him. He gives me a wolfish smile as his blue eyes take me in hungrily.

"You know you're mine and I love you, don't you?"

"Yes, Chance, yes, I'm yours," I pant.

"That's my good girl. Let that pussy come for me one more time. I want you with me."

He doesn't have to ask me too many times. As he kneads my ass and bounces me on his length, I come again with ease. I'm so wet it's louder than our panting.

"Fuck, I love you, baby," he groans in my ear as he reaches his own climax.

Chance

I've had way too much to drink tonight. I hadn't meant to fuck Jo like that against my truck, but I needed her. Feeling her pull away has been killing me.

I tug her head toward me to kiss it as I keep our fingers linked together while draping my arm around her. She looks up at me with that gorgeous smile on her lips. I can't help leaning in and nuzzling my nose against hers.

"I love you," I say against her lips before pecking them.

"I love you too. I just need to go to the bathroom. Be right back," she says with a shy smile.

I wink at her and let her go. As she walks away, I can't take my eyes off her. The sky could be falling, and I would still want her.

Nothing is going to change that for me. I can't wait for her to see the house. I've gotten the certificate of occupancy this week. Our home is ready. Peterson can kiss my ass.

No one will take our home from us. I've seen Jo sitting on our porch with a cup of hot chocolate a million times in my mind. I'm going to make that a reality. I promise I am.

My smile falls as Jo comes racing from the bathroom with anger and tears in her eyes. My mouth falls open, and I go to reach for her, but she bolts right by me. As the air flows through my fingers, it feels too real.

Like that's what I'm always grasping for, thin air. I don't know what just happened, but it's not good. I knit my brows in confusion.

What could have upset her that fast? We were fine only seconds ago. My mind races against the alcohol filling my system.

I'm not as sharp as I usually am. I palm my forehead then run my hand through my hair. I glance in the direction Jo went in to see her talking to Hersh and JC.

Still confused, I look back toward the restroom Jo came from. My heart aches as Lena and Ruby-Jean come out of the ladies room. My blood boils instantly.

"*Fuck, Fuck,*" I growl and turn to head for Jo.

CHAPTER SIXTEEN

Not What You Think

Jo

I couldn't wait to get out of that bar. I feel so stupid. It doesn't matter what Hershel says, this is on Chance.

He should have told me Lena was his ex. I shouldn't have had to find out while in a bathroom stall wiping his cum from between my legs. The part that kills me is the fact that Lena looked as horrified as I did when I stepped out of the stall.

At the time, I did my best to hold my head high as I washed my hands to leave that restroom with my dignity. I think I was in shock until I saw Chance's face. I keep hearing her friend over and over in my head.

"How are you holding up?"

"What do you mean?" Lena replied.

"I know it has to be killing you to see Chance with that Jo girl. I had such high hopes for you guys when you told me he hired you to work on his house. The two of you used to be so good together."

"Ruby-Jean, I—"

Lena's words cutoff as I walked out of the stall and her eyes went wide as she locked gazes with me in the mirror. I ignored them both as I washed my hands, but I didn't miss the smug look on Ruby-Jean's face as I turned to leave.

"Jo, right now I'm a little drunk but I promise we're going to talk about this in the morning," Mel says.

"We don't have to. I'm good."

"No, you're not and I'm not waiting to say something. Jo, at this point you're self-sabotaging. Lena is his ex as in from the past. You are that man's present and future.

"Hershel said this was years ago. Like junior high or high school or something. Could he have disclosed this? Yeah, he probably should have.

"Is it enough to throw away something good? Not at all. This isn't you," JC says.

"Nope, it's not. This is some JC shit," Mel huffs from the couch she's now sprawled on.

"I resent that. I hate it more because it's true and I wish like hell it wasn't. Jo, Mel is right.

"I see you taking on my bad habits. Being alone isn't for everyone. Shit, it isn't even for me. I was hurt a few times, and I became jaded.

"That was my path. I'm starting to see that everyone has a person. A right person who isn't going to hurt them and make them feel unwanted.

"Don't let my fucked-up way of thinking cause you to push away someone you love. If I had it all to do again, I'd live life a little differently," JC pleads.

"Well, damn, I guess I don't have to say shit. That sums up my Ted Talk. Jo, talk to your man. JC, follow your own advice.

"I have a mayor to save and a councilman breathing down my neck about some bullshit I still can't make sense of. Unless we're packing this show up and taking off for Japan or some shit, I'm calling it a night. I love you both."

With that, Mel closes her eyes and gets comfortable as she drags the throw blanket over her. I look at JC. She rolls her eyes and shakes her head.

The weight of the evening hits me. I stumble over to one of the accent chairs and flop down into it, dropping my head in my hands. My feelings are too hurt for me to think around them.

JC might be right but the alcohol in my system isn't allowing me to gather a single clear thought. Do I look up to my cousin? Yes. Have I tried to be more like her?

Lately, I find myself trying to take a page from her book when I want to guard my heart. If I would have stuck to that plan, I wouldn't be in this mess.

This was all a mistake. Tonight only proved how big a mistake it has been. My head is throbbing.

"Jo, baby girl—"

"I'm going to bed, Jodie. I heard you, but I need to go to bed."

"Stop overthinking. You've come such a long way."

I nod my head and get up to go shower. I need time to be alone. As I get to my room and peel my clothes off, my phone rings.

I sigh and think not to answer at all as I see its Marty. However, my drunken mind makes the decision for me. I pick up and flop down on the edge of my bed.

"Hey, Marty. What's up?"

"Oh, no. What's going on?"

"Nothing. Why do you always assume the worse?"

"I'm not assuming the worse. I just know you. You sound like someone stole your favorite snacks. We all know how grumpy you get when that happens."

I scoff. "I'm not that bad."

"Should I remind you how JC got that scar behind her ear?"

"Ugh, I never should have told you about that. Anyway. What's up? You're calling kind of late."

"I was thinking about you. We haven't talked in a minute. Usually when I call during the day you're working. On a ranch, might I add.

"What happened to all your big dreams? I thought that place was supposed to help you figure all that out, not turn you into some ranch hand," he rants.

"*Marty*," I drag out. "I've had too much to drink and this night has already been a shitshow. I can't do this right now."

"Trouble in paradise? You're seeing that guy, aren't you? I told you that wasn't a good idea."

"Marty, I haven't asked for you opinion on my love life," I bite out.

"Right, because I'm just the clean-up crew. You only listen to me after they show you, they ain't shit."

I jerk my head back and pull the phone from my ear. Marty has lost his fucking mind. It's not like I've dated a lot and I sure as shit haven't been running to him about my relationships.

Right now, his ass sounds delusional. I have never cried to him about my relationships, and I don't plan to start now. In fact, this isn't something I want to talk to anyone about.

"Jo, Jo."

My mouth drops open as Chance's voice boom through my mother's house. Her car was out front, so I do believe she's here tonight. Has everyone lost their minds?

"Marty, I need to go. You have a good night."

"Jo—"

I hang up before he can finish. We'll have a talk another time when I can think clearly. Right now, I need to get Chance's drunk ass up out of my mother's house.

Chance

Hershel was probably right. I should wait until the morning or at least until I'm fully sober before I talk to Jo. However, I can't allow this night to end without making this right.

"Jo. Jo," I call out.

Mel jumped up out of her sleep on the couch. I hadn't seen her there at first. JC appears looking confused and a moment later Jo runs out in a pink silk robe.

"What are you doing?" Jo whisper-yells.

"We need to talk. You left without allowing me to get a word in."

"Chance, your opportunity to explain anything was months ago. Now get out before you wake my mom."

"Baby, you're right. I should have told you about Lena. I just didn't think it was a big deal because it was junior high school.

"Jo, you know how I feel about you. You know I'm in love with you. Come on. Don't do this."

"Do what, Chance? You know what. Don't answer that. Just go."

"After the way we made love tonight, you really want to throw us away?"

"We didn't make love. I let you fuck me against your truck in a parking lot. You'll forget all about it like you forgot to tell me you used to date the woman you had help you with a house I've still never stepped foot in."

"Oh," Mel gasps as she clenches her imaginary pearls.

"Well damn," JC adds.

"You folks are grown, but you've lost your damn minds. Not in my woman's house, you don't. You're not going to have this out here tonight.

"Chance, get your butt on back to the inn. I raised you better than this. You and Jo can talk in the morning," Pop barks as he comes from the master bedroom with a sheet around his waist looking like he's about to pop us all with Mama's spoon.

I sigh and nod my head. "Sorry, Pop."

"Oh my God. This is so embarrassing," Jo gasps and runs off.

CHAPTER SEVENTEEN

Already Know

Jo

"Jo-jo Bell, I was hoping we'd get to talk before your mama gets up," Jack says as I walk into the kitchen.

I groan. "There's no way we can act like last night never happened?"

"Nope, not happening."

"Gah, you do know I used to like you," I groan.

He chuckles and pours me a cup of coffee in the mug beside him. Then he nods for me to take the seat beside him. I mope over and sit.

"I'm okay with you not liking me as long as you hear me. Me and your mama have been staying out of things for the most part. All of you youngins are old enough to figure your lives out.

"But what happened last night … Let me just say my boy isn't a fool but he sure is stupid for you. I talked to him this morning too and he filled me in on why he lost his damn mind coming up in here like that last night.

"Your sisters may have or might not have told your mama about what you believe to be true. Your mama was heartbroken, but she promised to wait for you to come to her. I see things a bit differently.

"I think you need to talk to your mama, stop making her wait you out, darlin'. That woman's love can heal a multitude of things and, Jo-jo Bell, you need some healing, baby girl. I'm saying this as a father and a friend.

"I want to see you happy, but I also don't want to watch my son get hurt. Everything Chance has done in the last seven or eight months has been for you. You might not be able to see it yet, but hiring Lena had more to do with you than anything else.

"That boy hasn't been romantically involved with Lena since he was a teenager. He had a job he needed done and because we're all working on saving this town, he hired her. She's from Spring Valley and still works and lives here.

"I think you know as well as I do that Chance is head over heels in love with you. However, sometimes when we're not dealing with our wounds, we start bleeding onto everything else. Take it from an old fool who almost lost the woman he loves.

"It's not worth the time you lose, Jo. Talk to your mama. Then go have a real talk with Chance."

"Okay, but can you keep it between us that I've been sleeping with your son?"

Jack bursts into laughter. "Oh, you're serious? You think we didn't already know? You kids are funny as hell."

"Aren't they?" Mom says as she comes into the kitchen, laughing and shaking her head. "Jo, I've known you and Chance have been in an intimate relationship since that boy couldn't stop smiling like a loon every time you entered a room. Heck, I was certain once you started working at the inn and following him around looking like a puppy lost in love."

"Why didn't you say anything?"

"Because you're a grown woman, Jo. I also know how much Chance cares for you. I also wanted to see how long you would keep sneaking around like you can't come talk to me," Mom says pointedly.

"I … I." I close my mouth and sigh. "I've been in therapy. I probably shouldn't have started a relationship with Chance until I resolved some things. You're right, Jack.

"I don't know that I'm truly angry at Chance about not telling me about Lena. It's just an excuse for me to pull away. To end things so bad things will stop happening."

"How would breaking up with the young man who has done nothing but bring a smile to your face have anything to do with anything?" Mom asks with furrowed brows.

"I know Mel and JC told you about why I'm seeing a therapist. I'm a jinx. I jinx love and people's happiness. It's been happening since I was a little girl.

"Chance and I were happy. It wasn't until I told him I love him that bad things started. Mr. Peterson, the delay with the spa, Chance not finding the right furniture for his place," I murmur.

Mom and Jack begin to chuckle. I look between the two confused. I can't think of what I've said that could be so funny.

"One of those things I'm not going to touch. Mr. Peterson is a lying ass. We'll leave him to the authorities.

"Your father is already on top of that. We haven't said anything because the situation has the potential to become dangerous, but no one is taking that land," Mom says.

"The spa delays are because I'm an old fart and I forgot to sign off on some things Chance left on my desk. I plan to give Chance the authority to make more final decisions so that doesn't happen again," Jack says.

"But—"

"But what, Jodie? You have always been a light in everyone's life. Never a burden or a jinx.

"I know the girls used to tease you and call you Jo the Jinx when you guys would play games, but it was never true. They were just mad they were getting beat by the baby. You've always been so smart for your age. You beat them at board games all the time.

"Listen to me. Your aunt loved you. She was very sick for a long time and hid it for almost as long. By the time we knew, she was at the end.

"Your friend Nancy moved because her father was abusive, and her mother had to get away and find help to stay safe. I helped them find help. Linda was the reason I started charity work to help abused women and children.

"Your father and I … we were becoming different people for a long time. Nothing and I do mean, *nothing* about our marriage fell apart because of you. If anything, we tried harder for you.

"In the end, we're happier as friends. We have you in common to talk and laugh about. We're both so proud of you. Jodie Ann, you could never be a jinx because you've been my lucky star from the day you were born," Mom finishes with tears in her eyes.

"Darlin', I promise you when you find out all that's been going on that you don't see, you're going to realize just how lucky you are. I know that smile and laugh have brightened things around here for me as much as your mama's presence has. Do you mind if I give you one more piece of advice?"

"No, sir."

"Letting go is so much more freeing than holding on to things that don't or can't add to your life in your present. Let that little girl put away those feelings and allow the woman you are today to be great," Jack says gentle.

I swipe at my tears and get up to give Mom a hug. She holds me tightly and whispers into my ear how much she loves me and how proud of me she is.

I release her and give Jack a hug. His warm embrace makes me want to call my dad. I didn't realize how attached I've become to Jack until now.

"Thanks, Jack. I still like you, by the way," I snicker.

"I love you, darlin'. I always wanted a daughter. I'm glad you're the closet thing I have to one. Don't go quitting on us before we make the finish line. I promise it will be worth it.

Chance

I'm a doer. There ain't no way I'm going to sit on my hands and allow Jo to slip through my fingers. I love her too much.

I tried that before, I'm not willing to go that route this time. Not when I know we're so good together. After talking to Pop this morning, I knew what my next step would be.

Now I'm here with a dozen roses clenched in one hand and dinner in the other. I plan to make this right once and for all. Once I get dinner and some candles set up, I'll be ready to lie it all bare.

"Hey, I wasn't sure if I would find you here, but I thought I would try."

I look up to find Lena standing on the porch of my home. Anger fills me and I get ready to rip her a new one, but she holds up her hands. I remember my mama and pop always telling me to treat a woman with gentle kindness and bite back my anger.

"I came to apologize for whatever trouble Ruby-Jean started. I didn't know Jo was in that stall and I didn't know Ruby-Jean was going to say any of that. I'm not around to start trouble.

"Everyone was having such a good time. The last thing I want is for everyone to find out how stupid I had been. Causing you guys any trouble would do just that," she tries to explain.

"This is my real life, Lena. You and Ruby-Jean might have cost me everything and for what?"

"I'm sorry. Let me talk to Jo. I can explain—"

"That's not your place. I fucked up. I should have told her about you.

"I didn't mean to make this bigger than it should be. Thanks for wanting to help, but I'll take care of things my own way."

"Chance, I … I'm really sorry," Lean says.

"Yeah, well—"

"Why'd you even ask me to come here?"

I turn at the sound of Jo's voice. I turn to look at Lena, then down at the roses and food in my hand. Fuck, I can see how this must look.

"Jo, wait," I call after her.

"Jo, please wait," Lena calls as she runs after Jo.

However, Jo is faster than us both. She jumps into her car and races off. I stumble to sit on the steps and drop my head.

"Un-fucking-believable. I can't catch a fucking break."

CHAPTER EIGHTEEN

Daddy's Girl

Jo

"There's my girl," Daddy croons as I come into view.

He stands from the table he's sitting at while waiting in the restaurant for me. It's so good to see him. I run right into his arms and hold on tight as he squeezes me.

"Hey, Daddy."

"How are you, sweetheart?"

"I've been better. How are you?"

"Come on and sit, we can get into all of that," he says warmly.

I take the seat across from his and settle in. He looks good, there's a sparkle in his eyes. I'm proud of how he and Mom have handled things.

"I wanted to be the first to tell you that Kennedy and I have been dating," he says.

"That's great, Daddy. Kennedy, that's your trainer from the gym, right?"

"She used to be my trainer. I've been training with Olly now."

"Will I get to meet her?"

He takes a pause and then a deep breath. I lift a brow because that's always his way of gearing up to say something he doesn't want to. I wait him out because I know he'll spit it out when he's ready.

"Kennedy is a bit younger than me. I wanted to see how you and your sisters feel about that," he says.

"Like how much younger?"

"Thirteen years."

"Dad, you're about to turn fifty. Wow, I mean, it's none of my business, but wow."

"We have a lot more in common than you would think. We haven't been dating long, but I'm hoping if things continue to go well, the two of you can meet."

"Then, you better keep her away from me for now," I mutter.

"Ah, I'm glad you opened that door for me. Talk to me, Jo. Why on earth would such a kind, talented, smart, and beautiful young woman believe she could be the cause of other's pain? What did we miss?"

"You didn't miss anything, Daddy. I mean, I know what love looks like. I know how it should feel.

"I've seen it all my life. My view is just a little skewed because of how close I was to people losing love. I'm trying. I really am," I say.

"If you know what love looks like, how are you missing how much Chance loves you?"

"How do you know about that?" I murmur.

"Jack and I have become friends. We speak a lot and Chance and I may have spoken a time or two."

I sigh heavily. "I haven't missed that he loves me, but you can't say one thing and do another. Daddy, I've been cheated on. I'm not about to go through that again, especially not with someone I love."

"Jo, why do you think Chance cheated on you or would?"

"I … I. He invited me to his new place, and she was there."

"The ex-girlfriend from junior high. The one who he fired because she made you upset. Are we speaking of the same young lady?"

"Yeah, I guess."

"You're my daughter. I think you already know I'd hurt a motherfucker about you. Put up all the suits, throw away all the proper shit. You're my baby. You come from my loins.

"I'm not going to tell you to break yourself for no man. Not ever. What I will say is that I think you might want to take a deeper look at what's going on around you.

"Chance made one mistake that came from a good place. He didn't cheat and it was never his intension to hurt you. The night he invited you over, he had a surprise set up for you. The young lady showed up to apologize just before you arrived."

"Dad, I just don't want to keep people pleasing and forgetting about myself. I've pushed me aside all my life thinking if I breathe wrong, I'd lose someone and too afraid to allow anyone new too close.

"I'm just feeling like maybe I'm losing myself somehow. I jumped right into Chance's plan to help, and it somehow became my thing too. What about my plans? What about my—"

He laughs cutting me off. I look at him feeling confused. He reaches across the table and covers my hand.

"Jo, you're so stubborn when you want to be. I know you're here in the city because you're running from your boyfriend. I also know you have a whole lot you're walking away from for a misunderstanding. Have I ever let you down?"

"No," I mumble.

"Then, trust me. Your dreams aren't going unactualized. Your mother, Jack, and I are proud of you two and all you've done in Spring Valley. See your work through, Jodie. I'm not just talking about the ranch either.

"I want to celebrate with you when you overcome this false belief you have. My magical girl. Did you know I took and passed the bar the week after you were born.

"Hadn't slept for shit and had your pacifier clipped to my shirt. Which your mom was pissed about. Took her hours to find the extras I had put away," he chuckles.

"Really?"

"Yes, really. For the next four months you were like my own personal volume. I held you close and prayed that I'd pass that exam to give you everything you wanted and deserved.

"I'd say you're the least jinxed person there is. You're just a gorgeous young lady full of deep empathy. Empathy your young mind didn't know how to handle and I'm so sorry, we didn't catch on or see that.

"Baby, amazing things are happening all around you because of that big heart of yours. You just need to show patience and understanding. You now have someone else who's praying to give you all the same things I wanted for you," he says.

I nod. "Thanks, Dad. I don't know why, but I think I needed to hear this from you."

"Because I'm kind of awesome and I've always been your hero."

"Never a lie told. You're the best, Dad."

"I'm proud of all you girls, but you know you're my star. Now, let's get something to eat, yeah?"

With that, he lifts his hand and waves the waitress over for us to order. I sit and allow his words to sink in. The one thing I'm hearing loud and clear from everyone is that I don't have a full picture. In fact, I never do. Not as a child and not now as an adult.

The difference now is I have the option to get all the facts to grasp the larger view. I've talked more with JC, and I see a lot of things differently now. I thought I knew so much from looking from the outside in.

What am I missing with Chance?

Chance

"Bro, you have to stop looking so nervous," JC laughs as we ride in the car to the bar Jo and her friends are at.

I am nervous. Jo has no idea I'm here in the city. I'm on her turf this time.

"He is nervous. Girl, I knew we were bringing him here, but I didn't know you were going to give him a makeover," Mel scoff.

I got in while Mel was at her office here. JC took me to buy new clothes and to get a haircut. I even got new cologne.

It's a far cry from the T-shirts and jeans Jo is used to seeing me in. I look more like a model about to walk the runaway. I have no idea how Jo is going to feel about any of this.

However, I do feel confident about what I've come here to do. I know what I want and I'm here to get just that. Jo can run all she wants, but we belong together and I'm here to make sure she knows that.

"He looks like a freaking GQ model. I did my thing. Thank you very much," JC sings.

"That you did. You look handsome, Chance. Relax, babe. Jo's little stubborn ass will stop to listen tonight. I can promise you that."

"I hope you're right, Mel. It's only been a few days, but it feels like forever."

"I can't wait until she realizes you built that house for her, and you were trying to give it to her the other night."

"I still want to bop Lena upside her damn head. I know she didn't mean for any of this to happen, but damn she can't buy a clue and her timing is ass," JC says.

"I agree on her having the worse timing," I snort.

"Well, your big sisters are here to help you fix this. You're a good guy, Chance. I know you're not going to make me regret this. But just in case I'm wrong, you should know I hide the bodies for my employers. Don't become a body, Chance," Mel leans to whisper in my ear. I glance at the driver upfront and then look back to her.

She laughs and pats my cheek. I turn to JC and she only winks. I shake my head, I feel sorry for anyone who tries to cross the two of them.

"We're here," Mel croons. "Showtime. Come on handsome, let's get your girl back home."

"I'm all for that. This city is starting to make me itch," JC grumbles.

"You too?"

"We should probably tell Mom to sell the house."

"Let's talk to Jo first," Mel says.

"You guys thinking of moving to Spring Valley too?"

"Honey, keep up. We're there more than we're here. Some of us already made the move," Mel says.

I keep my mouth shut as it's none of my business. I've heard a thing or two, but now isn't the time for me to pry. I have my own business to handle inside.

CHAPTER NINETEEN

Face Me

Jo

I've felt so free after my lunch with my dad today. However, something has become very clear since I've been in the city this time. This doesn't feel like home anymore.

When Marty found out I was here, he insisted I come out for drinks with him and a few of our friends. I thought that would help me feel at home somehow, but it hasn't. Don't get me wrong, we've been having such a blast.

I've been carefree and focused on having fun, but that feeling just isn't there. I feel like my body is here, but my mind and heart are somewhere else.

JC and Mel said they would probably stop by, but I'm not counting on that. They're probably packing to head back already. None of us stay here for long anymore.

"Jo, don't look now, but Jarold is here," Sonia whispers in my ear.

"No," I whine and stomp my foot.

I'm having fun. I don't want to deal with my ex. I grab another shot and throw it back.

"Dance with me," I sing as I grab Bell by the hand and drag her with me.

We make our way out to the small dance floor as the bass from the up-tempo beat vibrates through the floors. I throw myself into the music and forget all about Jarold. That is until Marty comes over and places himself protectively in front of me.

I look to see Jarold had been making his way toward me. I look up at Marty and give him a smile. He winks back at me.

"Thanks, bestie," I call over the music.

We all continue to dance and have fun. I'm lost in the music until the DJ kills the vibe as he transitions into a slow song. I snort as "Stay" by Tyrese comes on.

I go to walk back to the table our friends are surrounding. Suddenly, I feel eyes on me. I turn thinking I'll find Jarold, but I find the last person I thought I would see tonight.

Chance is standing in this bar looking like a whole snack. Damn, damn, damn. Where the hell did this come from?

He's dressed in a black dress shirt that's tucked into a pair of high waisted wide leg pants. The shirt has a few buttons open, and something seems different about his hair.

I can't really see from this distance in this low lighting, but whatever it is seems to be drawing attention to his sharp features. I bite my lip as I allow my gaze to take him in from head to toe.

"Jo, wait. Stay and dance with me," Marty whispers in my ear as he captures my arm.

"I can't. He's here for me. He's always here for me." I shake my head and pull away until he frees my arm.

"What? Who? You can't be talking about Jarold. He—"

"No, not him," I say and walk away.

Chance waits for me to get to him, holding his arms open when I get about a foot away. I rush into his arms and hug his waist. Oh my God, he smells so good.

It's not his usual cologne. It's something new and so fucking delicious smelling. I bury my face in his chest and inhale deeply.

He palms the side of my face, tilting my head back and then devours my lips. I lift onto my toes and wrap my arms around his neck. It feels like coming home.

"I love you," he breathes into my mouth.

"I know," I moan. "This isn't my home anymore. I want to go back with you."

"Good, because our life is waiting. Jodie?"

"Yeah?"

He grabs ahold of my hand and gives it a squeeze. I look up into his eyes, searching. This feels right. I'm not fighting my feelings for once and it feels like the right thing.

"I'm going to ask you now before something else can get in the way." He reaches into his pocket, then leans into my ear. "Will you marry me?"

The next thing I know, he's in the middle of this bar on one knee. I gasp and cover my mouth in shock. My conversation with my father comes back to me.

This is why he and Chance have spoken. He was going to propose. I nod my head and fling myself at him.

Chance lifts to his full height taking me with him as I wrap my legs around his waist. He palms the back of my head and kisses me like it's the last time he'll ever get the chance to. I give back just as good as I'm getting.

"I love you, baby. It's always been you. Only you. I'm going to make you so happy."

"I love you too, Chance. I'm sorry. I love you so much."

"Yes, that's what I'm talking about, killer. Get your woman."

I hear Mel squealing before I can place eyes on her. Chance places me back on my feet and I turn to find Mel and JC with huge smiles on their faces as they look back at me. I guess everyone knew a lot more than I did.

Thank you, I mouth to my sisters. They both rush over and pull me into a hug. The sound of glass crashing to the floor grabs everyone's attention.

I'm shocked to find Jarold pinning Marty to a wall by his collar. There's a table knocked over, and beer bottles shattered on the floor. Marty looks pissed and shocked.

Two of Jarold's friends rush to get him off Marty. He releases Marty but only after shoving him away hard. I can't hear what he growls at Marty, but his face is filled with rage as he storms out.

I notice Bell—who's closest to where the confrontation is happening—with a strange look on her face. She shakes her head, glares at Marty and then storms away too. I'm too stunned to make sense of any of it.

"*O … kay*," Mel drags out.

"What was that about?" JC asks.

"I have no idea," I murmur.

"How about I buy a round for everyone? We have celebrating to do. I asked my best friend to marry me, and she said yes," Chance croons.

"Now that's how you get out of the friendzone," Mel cheers.

"I got a hundred bucks that says Jack and Mom are next," JC says.

"I'm not giving away no money. I'd sooner bet on you and Hershel having a baby than take that ass bet."

"Well, at least you know Chance is still going to be fit in his old age. Did you see Jack come out in that sheet ready to knock heads about y'all disrespecting his woman's house," JC snickers.

"I thought I was the only one who caught that one," Mel laughs.

"Nope."

"Hey, ladies. That's still my pop. I can only hope to stay in shape like that. Hopefully running the ranch with my wife will keep me in shape."

"If it doesn't interfere with me starting my own spa," I tease.

"*Oow*, you're the smartest dummy I know," JC barks and laughs.

"What?"

"Nothing, boo. We love you just as you are," Mel croons.

"What did I miss?" I ask and look at Chance.

He leans in to peck the tip of my nose. "Nothing, darlin'. You'll have your business, and you can still make beer with me. We'll have it all, I promise."

I smile happily as I look up at him. He leans in to nuzzle my neck as he pulls me in close. I'm so freaking happy right now.

Chance

"Good night you two, we'll have breakfast in the morning to celebrate while you call Mom and give her and Jack the news," JC calls as Jo takes me by the hand to lead me up the stairs.

"See you guys in the morning," Jo sings drunkenly over her shoulder.

I quicken my steps and glide my hand over her side and around her waist from behind. As we get to the top of the landing, I pull her back against my front and bury my face in her neck.

Jo reaches up to hold me bent over her as she turns her face up to mine. Quickly, I capture her lips as I rock from side to side with her in my embrace. My heart couldn't be more filled with love than it is now.

"I'm so glad you're here. I talked to my dad earlier and I had planned to go back home in the morning," she says into the kiss.

"Home?"

"Yes, home. Where you are is where I belong. I can second guess everything and be wrong or I can live and be happy. I'm choosing you, because I'm always happy when I'm with you. Well, most of the time," she laughs.

"I never want to see you unhappy. I promise I'll do everything in my power so that I never do again."

"I know what would make me really happy," she purrs.

"What's that, baby?"

"Having my fiancé take me in my room to have hot, drunken sex tonight."

"And which door is that?"

Her fiancé, we're engaged. She said yes. Jo is going to be my wife.

It took everything in me not to throw her over my shoulder and carry her out of that bar. For hours, I've wanted to bring her back here to the house where we could be alone. Her friends were all cool except for that Marty guy.

He was cold to me and ended up leaving not long after I bought everyone a round. Jo shrugged it off and so did I. Nothing can ruin my night after my girl said yes.

I've never seen Jo happier. She hasn't stopped smiling at me. To be honest, my smile hasn't left my face either. From the time we walked into the bar, I was captivated by her.

She looked so sexy in the black high waisted skirt and silver crop top. I couldn't help growing hard as I stood there watching her on the dance floor. She looked so relaxed and carefree.

Now all I can think about is getting her out of this skirt and top and having my way with her body all night. The more I think about her being my fiancée, the more I want to have her walls wrapped around me.

"It's this one," she says as she takes me by the hand again and tugs me through a door on the left.

I close the door behind me before tugging Jo into my arms. We kiss passionately as she works on the buttons of my shirt while I pull down the zipper on her skirt.

I chuckle as she fumbles with my belt. Releasing her, I reach to slowly take off the belt, putting on a show for her. I haven't missed the way she's been eyeing me all night.

JC was right, Jo is into this look. Her eyes fill with lust as she watches my every movement. I toss the belt aside and then go to take off the black dress boots.

Jo bites her lip as she gives an appreciative nod. Once my boots are off, I straighten to my full height and go to remove my pants. Jo makes a tsking sound and shakes her head.

I drop my arms to my sides and lift a brow at her. She moves to the vanity in the room and picks up a hair tie. She then pulls her hair into a ponytail as she moves back toward me.

I remain silent as I take her in. She stops before me and looks up at me through her lashes, still biting her lower lip. I cup the side of her face and pull her lip free before running my thumb across it.

"You're so gorgeous," I murmur.

"I was thinking the same thing. I love this look on you," she says as she reaches into my shirt and runs her hands over my torso.

Her small hands are so warm and soft. I can't help tugging her in for a kiss. I take her lips in a searing connection as I pull her in closer.

She moans into my mouth as she pushes my shirt from my shoulders and then runs her hands over my biceps. I find the fastenings for her top and release them.

However, she pulls away and gets rid of the garment before I can. I groan and lift her in my arms to carry her over to the bed. I place her down gently and begin to kiss my way down her body slowly.

"Chance," she cries out and bows off the bed.

I take my time to kiss between the valley of her breasts and down her stomach. Adding my tongue as I taste and tease her flesh. Looking up her body, I can see her watching me.

This woman who once had no clue how much I wanted her is now lying here beneath me looking as if she wants me just as much if not more. I'm glad I didn't give up. Jo is worth it. She's so much stronger than she knows and getting stronger.

"Tell me what you want, baby. How do you want me to fuck you first?"

"Keep taking charge. I know you'll get us there," she says with enough trust to cripple me.

I nod my head, still not taking my eyes off hers as I spread her open and dive in. She cries out and reaches for the top of my hair to lock her fingers in. In this moment, I'm glad we kept the length on top.

"Fuck, Chance. Shit, that feels so good," she whimpers.

I reach to cover her hand she's fisting the sheets with. When her legs begin to tremble, I groan. I reach down into my pants to squeeze myself for some relief. I've never wanted her more.

I begin to work on getting my pants off as she comes down from her orgasm. However, Jo sits up quickly and reaches to pull my zipper down. She then shoves the pants and my boxer briefs down.

Needing some relief, I palm my length and begin to stroke. Jo runs her hands over my abs and back down over my thighs. I grin as she gets that look on her face.

I know what comes next. She knocks my hand away and takes me into her mouth. I drop my head back and groan.

I can do this for the rest of my life. Exploring sex with Jo has been an eye opening experience. I thought I was experienced before I met her.

However, I have to wonder who's teaching who? I've learned things about myself and what I truly like. I think that's what I love most about Jo.

I'm experiencing life with her. This isn't a one-way road where I decide everything. Yes, I've tried to take the lead, but in every step we've taken I've learned something new about myself, about her, and about us.

Just when I don't think I can hold back another second, Jo brings me to my knees. I fall against the bed as she laughs to herself. I recover enough to kick my pants from my feet and settle on my back on the mattress.

Jo comes to lie beside me. I reach for her face and wipe the cum from the corner of her mouth. She takes my hand and sucks my thumb between her lips, humming as she locks eyes with me.

I give her a smile and tug her face to mine. As we kiss, Jo reaches to bring me back to life. I'm hard in no time.

"Chance," she moans as she climbs over me and settles on my length.

"You look so gorgeous when you're riding me. You were made just for me, Jodie."

"I know. This is the only place I want to be. With you for the rest of my life."

Those words ignite a fire within me. I lift up until we're nose to nose and flip her onto her back. With each thrust into her soft, tight body, I feel my life connecting to hers. I can't imagine being without her … ever.

CHAPTER TWENTY

Home Sweet Home

Jo

"I thought we were going to stay at the inn. Mom and Jack are already back and I wanted to spend the night together," I purr as Chance turns for Willowbrook.

"We don't have to stay at the inn anymore. I have something I want to show you," he says as he squeezes the thigh his hand is resting on.

"*O … kay,*" I drag out.

I go back to texting with Bell. She's been texting a lot since the other night. I'm not sure what's going on between her and Marty, but she's been asking me a ton of questions about him.

A text comes in from my dad, bringing a smile to my face. I think my parents are happier than I am about me getting married. Mom and Jack were so happy for us when we called with the news.

I'd thought we would come right back to Spring Valley that next morning, but everyone else had other plans. I thought Mel and JC were taking us out to brunch, which was crazy after the breakfast JC made while I made my phone calls. However, I went along with it because everyone was so happy.

I didn't even pay attention to how weird my father acted when I spoke to him on the phone. It was only after we arrived at brunch that I realized everyone was in the city. Mom, Jack, Hershel, Cash, and Emma were all in the restaurant when we arrived.

Dad and his girlfriend Kennedy were there too. The engagement brunch was just what we needed. It was like a blessing from both our families.

I could see how happy everyone was for us. Including myself for me. Every time I caught our reflections in the mirrors the smiles on our faces said it all.

It was good to see both my parents happy and to see the friendships their new partners have with them and their partners. It was a happy moment for us all. After two more days in the city, we're finally back.

I look up as the car stops. Chance drove my car back since he didn't drive in to see me. I snap my head in his direction when I see we're in front of his new house.

"I've been dying to show you this place. Come on," he says excitedly.

He jumps out and rounds the car to open my door. I grab the hand he offers and step out. His excitement is bouncing off him.

I follow him up onto the porch and smile at the porch swing. There are throw pillows on it with C&J embordered on them. Before I can allow that to sink in, Chance opens the door, then turns to scoop me up and carries me inside.

The foyer is as gorgeous as the one at Mom's. However, the window over the door allows a ton of light in. Chance places me on my feet and I spin around taking it all in.

"This place is amazing, Chance. Wow, it came out so nice. Congratulations."

"Go on, walk through. Take it all in," he says with a huge smile.

I nod and start to move through the house. I find a couple of cute secondary bedrooms and can't help imagining our little family here. However, it's when I get to the master bedroom that I notice something.

"This is the furniture I liked. When you couldn't decide what you wanted, this was the one I said I thought was nice," I gasp.

"Come, there's more," he says.

I turn and follow him to the living room and note the same thing. It's all the furniture I said I liked. However, he doesn't stop there.

He takes me through the house to the above ground basement. There is a second kitchen here, a popcorn machine, and a snack area. When he leads me through a door and I see it's a theater room, I squeal and turn to look at him.

He gives me a huge smile. I run into his arms and hold him tight as he lifts me onto his waist. He kisses the side of my head.

"Did I get it right?"

"Chance, what are you saying?"

"I've been building this house for you all this time. For our family. It was supposed to be a surprise, but that didn't work out the way I wanted it to. Not really."

I press my forehead to his. "You were building this place for me?"

He places me back on my feet and stares down into my eyes. It feels like this is the most intimate moment we've ever had. I'm stunned that he has done this for me.

As it's all setting in, I can see our talks and ideas throughout the parts of the house I've walked through. As if reading my mind, his next words confirm my thoughts.

"Yes, this has always been your house. Every detail has been designed with you in mind. With our future in mind. From the secret playroom for our girls to the hidden boys' club for our boys.

"Their game room is sick. Me and Hershel will break it in for them. I even made sure our master bath is spa like.

"This is my engagement gift to you, baby. This and the spa at the ranch."

"The spa at the ranch?" I say knitting my brows in confusion.

"Yes, it's yours. We're going to build your business together. I don't just want you to manage it until you find your next thing,

I want you to own it with me. The spa, the ranch, the brewery, it's all ours."

"Chance, I thought you were just expanding the business. I didn't know you wanted to build my business with me."

"That's all I ever wanted, Jo. You pulled me into your dreams with every talk we had. Suddenly, my dreams and yours made sense together.

"You were the best friend I didn't know I needed but the one I can't live without. I've been able to see us as a team from the beginning."

"That's why you've always been so sure about us? It's been your plan all along and when you plan something you follow through," I murmur.

"Is that a problem, babe?"

"No, it's one of the things I love about you. It's something I've admired from the beginning."

"In the beginning, I had no idea about your fears. All I did know was that you were amazing and I loved you.

"I want to be the one you dream with and create with. Your mom told me if I showed you the way, you would get there with me on your own."

I nod my head. "She was right. All this time I've been spending here in Spring Valley has gotten me here with you wholeheartedly. This truly feels like home, Chance.

"That little voice is still whispering that I'll mess it all up somehow, but I'm listening to my heart. This is where I belong and I can't wait to be your wife."

"This land has been in my family for generations. Each Harrington has had a chance to build their own legacy. It's my turn and I plan to do that with you until the day you don't want to be by my side anymore.

"Through the good and the bad I'm going to be right here, Jo. There's nothing you can do to jinx this. I'm not weak of heart.

"I'm not going to give up on you, abuse your love or your trust, or take your feeling of security from you. I want to be your best friend for the rest of your life like my daddy was to my mama, and how your daddy is to your mama."

I cup the side of his face. I'm in awe of how well he understands my feelings. Deep down inside, I know these aren't just words. Chance means them all.

"I love you. Do you want to show me the master bedroom again?"

"I thought you'd never ask. I love you too."

With that, he tosses me over his shoulder and heads back through the house. I can't help the smile on my face as I have an upside-down view of my new home. Our home.

Chance

I wake naked and thirsty. Blinking a few times, as I try to push the sleep aside. Instantly, I'm bombarded with memories of our first night in our new home together.

I reach out for Jo but find her side of the bed cold and empty. Realizing she isn't in bed with me any longer, I sit up and look around. Everything seems to be so quiet and still, drawing my attention to the rain dancing on the roof of the house.

Climbing out of bed, I then head into my closet for a pair of basketball shorts or some sweats. I get my hands on a pair of shorts first and tug them on. Doubling back into the bedroom, I grab my phone before I go in search for Jo.

"Jo," I call out.

I don't get a reply, but I note the lights that are on throughout the house. I follow them upstairs and smile. I think I know where I'm going to find her.

I reach for the latch on the hidden door, amused that Jo might have found it on her own. I placed it right where she said it should be. Once the door is open, I move inside and climb the stairs.

I find Jo sitting on one of the beanbags with a book clenched to her chest as she stares up at the skylight. With a smile on my lips, I lean against the wall and watch her. The movement seems to grab her attention.

"Everything okay?"

"Yeah, just thinking."

"About?"

"You, this, us. I mean, all those times I thought we were just talking. I've always thought that you were listening, but not like this.

"You got it down to every single detail I mentioned. I remember telling you about the reading room Dad made for us and how I wanted one for my girls so they could know what it was like to have a daddy who listened to their dreams and helped them to find their own.

"A place where they would want to invite us in when they are little and a safe place to escape when they get older. The twinkle lights, the bookshelves, that's a skylight balcony, isn't it?"

"Yes, darlin', it is. I listened to every detail. Every single word," I reply.

"I never thought I would find someone to love me this much. To love our children as much as my dad loved us but look. This room is filled with so much love, and our girls aren't even here yet.

"Look at how much you love them. Heck, we could have a house full of boys," she snorts a laugh and sniffles.

"Then this room will be all yours. Your escape from all the chaos my boys are sure to cause," I chuckle.

"Come sit with me. This room is so peaceful. I can't believe you filled the shelves with my favorite childhood books."

"Your mother was very instrumental in compiling that list," I say as I move to sit behind her. Jo moves around until we both settle into place, her between my legs as I wrap my arms around her.

"Can I ask you something?"

"Go on. I'm an open book."

"What were you going to do if I couldn't get there with you?"

"I would have still been your best friend, and this would have been my Christmas gift to you. A place of your own next to your mom. The chance to build up to your next step."

"I think I like this option better. Boys or girls our children are some lucky kids. This place is amazing, Chance. Thank you for listening to me."

"No problem, baby. Like I said it's all a part of my dreams too," I say and kiss the top of her head.

We fall into silence as the rain continues to pound the roof and the skylight. I've never felt more peaceful in my life. This is what I envisioned when I thought of this room.

I did it. I made the perfect world for us. I can feel how happy Jo is and that's all I ever wanted. Her happy and in my life.

Just when I feel like I'm about to nod off Jo's phone rings, but she can't get her hands on it before it goes to voice mail. Then mine begins. Looking at the time, I furrow my brows. Something is up.

"Hello. Pop, is everything okay?"

"Where are you and Jo?"

"We're at the house. What's going on?"

"Thank God," he breathes.

"*Dad,*" I drag out.

"The alarm system at the house in the city was tripped and there has been some threatening calls. We just wanted to make sure you and Jo are all right."

"Threatening calls? To who? From who?"

"We have it under control. I just want you and Jo to keep your distance from Peterson. He's dangerous. I can't say if this is connected to him, but we're working on it."

"We who, Pop?"

"I can't say much right now. Just listen to what I said. You and Jo stay away from him."

"Well, have the authorities been to the house? Is everything all right there? Have Mel and JC made it back yet?"

"They're both at Willowbrook with Coral. I'm heading that way now."

"All right, Jo and I will be right over."

"You can come over in the morning. I'm just going to lay eyes on Coral for myself. I knew this would happen," he says.

"What aren't you telling me, Pop."

"All that bullshit going on with Cash and Peterson showing up when he did, it's all connected. Like I said. I can't say more now. We'll talk in the morning, son."

"Be safe, Pop. I don't like how any of this sounds."

"You have nothing to worry about. I'm still a bull they don't want to get in the ring with. When it comes to my family and my land, I see nothing but red.

"I'm not going to be bullied into or out of shit that's mine. I need to go. You stay safe too, son."

"Love you, Pop."

"I love you too, Chance."

CHAPTER TWENTY-ONE

Crazy

Jo

I take a sip of water and sigh. I haven't been feeling too hot today, but I'm pushing through. I have to it's the grand opening of the spa.

"This was such a good idea. This turnout has been awesome. I've barely had time for a break until now," Bell says as she appears from the back area.

"You're telling me. Those demos went over great. Everyone was so excited. So far, you've been booked for every day you'll be in town."

"Well, bring it on. This place has such a good vibe. I feel like I'm at a mix of home and my best friend's house. Besides, you guys have some great tippers."

I smile proudly. It was Chance's idea to move our grand opening the weekend of the Christmas party the B&B is throwing for the town. Bell will be staying with us for the next two weeks.

She arrived yesterday to walk the spa and help prepare for today. I've seen the look in her eyes. Spring Valley's magic may have captured another one.

I would love if she came to work here for us. I'm grateful to her and my other co-workers who came out for this event. We're still hiring permanent staff.

I want to make sure we get this right. However, we did need the help to pull this all off as I saw it in my head. I'm so happy with the results.

"Well, that was it for today. Chance is setting up lunch for the team. Let's turn the place for tomorrow and we can head over," I say.

"Sounds good. I heard Joey mention to someone he's thinking of signing a six-month contract and looking for a place in town to live. He wants to see if this is a fit. I'm totally in if he does," Bell says.

"Really?" I say excitedly.

"Heck yeah. Joey is a vibe. Not to mention his older brother tends to be a fixture in this life. I'm all about getting to know more about him. Besides, you and Joey are like my last cool friends to hang out with."

"Speaking of which, what was going on with you and Marty?"

I'm genuinely curious. Marty hasn't been calling me as much and I'm not sure he'll show this weekend, like he said he would originally. When I do talk to him it's been a bit strained.

"You still don't know, do you?"

"Know what?"

"Marty isn't the friend you think he is. Shit … I told him he needed to tell you this, but it looks like he's still on some bullshit."

"Bell, what are you talking about?"

"I overheard what Jarold said to Marty that night after your proposal. I was curious and did some digging to find out the truth. Not to break you and Chance up or anything, but because if I heard right that was some fucked up shit," she says.

"What did Jarold say?"

"He told Marty 'you did this' after he shoved him. I was confused but I started to think about all the times Jarold showed up at the Spa wanting to speak to you. You told me that Marty sent you the video that lead to the breakup.

"So I confronted him about it. Of course he lied, but I ran into Jarold a week or so later. He told a very different story."

"But he didn't deny it when I called him to confront him," I say in confusion.

"According to Jarold, you called him in the middle of something at work. He was caught off guard and his boss walked in so he couldn't really respond. Listen, I had my cousin run the video through one of those AI checker.

"That shit was faker than RuPaul's wigs. You do know Marty works for that IT company. This isn't something hard for him to do.

"When I confronted him again, he swore he would come clean and tell you. I told him if he didn't, I would. I haven't spoken to him since because I hate what he did," she finishes.

"Wait, why would he do something like this?"

"Jo, I've known you for a long time. There are a ton of guys who have had a thing for you, and I don't think you ever notice. Marty has been one of those guys.

"He's been willing to do anything to get close to you. Pretend to be feminine to be your bestie, moving into your neighborhood when I don't think he could afford it at the time, and now break up your relationship in hopes you'd run into his arms."

"Oh my God," I gasp and clench my stomach. "I think I'm going to be sick."

"I'm so sorry, honey."

"No, I'm glad I know. This is crazy."

Marty

I hadn't planned to come all this way. I was going to let Jo go. However, the more I thought about it, the more I can't.

I worked so hard to get her to see me. I've been everything to her. I waited for her to be ready to date.

I thought I would be her first choice. The way she smiles at me, the way she laughs. We've always had a connection. Then she started to date that Jarold guy.

I put up with it. I was going to allow her her fun. Then she started to talk about him like he was so great. She was going to introduce him to her parents.

"Not on my fucking watch," I snarl as I sit in my car staring at Jo and Bell as they walk into the barn where the Christmas party is being held.

That fucking nosy bitch Bell ruined everything. I had planned to set this new guy up just like I did Jarold. All I needed was more information on him.

I knew she was seeing him before he showed up and proposed to my girl. I almost had enough to make him look like the worse man on earth. I figured that's Jo's trigger, cheating men.

I've been faithful to her all this time. I'm loyal to a fault. Even when she started dating, I remained loyal.

I'm all hers. Now she's giving everything to someone else and I'm here on the outside looking in. That stops tonight.

This guy has built her dream for her, but I'm going to watch it all burn. When there's nothing left here for her to run to, she'll come back to the city, and I can fix things.

"Bell has to go. You need to get rid of Bell before she ruins everything."

Yes, that's the plan. I'll just wait until I can get to Bell and then I'll turn it all to ashes. I'm tired of waiting on the sidelines for Jo to notice me.

This is the end.

Jo

My stomach has been unsettled since my conversation with Bell earlier. I'm still in such disbelief. If not for Marty, Chance and I wouldn't be together.

I don't know how to feel about that. I don't regret my relationship with Chance, but I don't think what Marty did was fair to me or Jarold. He manipulated my life.

I feel my stomach turn every time I think about it. To be honest, I don't know how I made it through tonight. I'm in the office of the barn trying to catch my breath. I don't want to ruin Mom and Jack's night.

The party has ended and almost everyone has left. Mom and Jack have been dancing together lost in their own little bubble. I'm so happy for them.

It will be so much fun to help Mom plan her wedding as I plan mine. Chance and I have already decided we're going to hold the wedding here on the ranch. I've thought about having the ceremony by the lake and the reception right here in the barn where we've been hosting events.

Or we could have everything in our own backyard. I look forward to the happy times. Time when I can put all the betrayal behind me.

"Are you ready to go?" Chance says as he wraps his arms around me.

I sink back into his embrace and sigh. This is my safe place. All the crazy out there can't touch us.

"Can we leave, is everything cleaned up? I want to get it all done tonight so it's not on my mind in the morning when I open the spa," I say.

"The band is still loading up to leave. I'm waiting for Sherman to get back so I can pay them. Hershel, Mel, and JC are finishing up.

"I think Cash is giving them a hand before he heads out. I gave Bell my keys to the Spa. She thinks she left something there this afternoon.

"We can head out as soon as she gets back. Are you feeling okay? I can draw you a bath when we get home," he says.

"That would be nice. It's been a long day. I think I just need to lie down for a bit, and I'll be okay."

He kisses my neck and tightens his hold around me. I bask in the feel of his arms. We've been living together for almost two months now.

To say I'm comfortable in his arms is an understatement. Our family has only gotten stronger in the last year. Mr. Peterson is a thing of the past and our future here on the ranch is more than secure.

"Jo? I have a question for you."

"Okay. What's up?"

"Is it possible you're pregnant? Your cycle hasn't come this month, and it should have by now. We have been a little reckless with drinking and having unprotected sex in the last few months.

"I'm just thinking. We couldn't have gotten so lucky so many times. Maybe you're not feeling well because—"

He doesn't get to finish his words as my stomach rolls, and I reach for my bag and take off. It's as if my body is answering the question for him. I'm not going to make it to the inn, but I dart straight for the spa. Chance said Bell is there.

"Jo, wait," Chance calls out from behind me, but I can't stop.

My mouth is watering, and I don't think I can make it stop this time. I can use one of the restrooms inside. I pray that I'll make it in time.

I don't want to ruin this purse by having to heave into it. However, that's my plan if I don't make it. As I race for the bathroom, I think of what Chance said.

He's not wrong. We've had unprotected sex after a night of drinking a few times, starting with that one night in the parking lot of Luke's. We've been pushing it.

If I'm not pregnant that would be a shock. I don't know why I didn't think of that earlier. I guess my mind has been preoccupied with so many other things.

There's been the move, the grand opening, finding employees, Jack asking me and my sisters for our blessing to marry Mom. Then there's all the other things that have been going on around us. It's like one thing settles and something else turns up.

I tug the front door open and rush inside, making it to the bathroom just in time to double over the toilet. I empty my stomach as tears burn the backs of my eyes. Once this sick feeling passes, I know they will be tears of joy.

I'm going to be a mom. Now that the idea is setting in, I'll be so disappointed if I'm not. Chance will make such a great father.

I want this more than anything. I know running the ranch and having a baby isn't going to be easy, but we have the support. It will be okay.

My heart blooms with happiness. I have my luxury spa business, I'm getting married, and now I'm having a baby.

"Jo, where are—"

I frown as Chance's words cut off, and the scent of smoke fills the air. What the hell?

Chance

I'm in shock. I had only asked the question out of curiosity, but something tells me I might be right. I stand staring after Jo as she runs from the office.

After a few seconds I snap out of it and run after her. If she's going to be sick, I want to be there for her. If she's upset because I asked if she's pregnant, we need to have a real talk.

"Jo, wait," I call out as I run after her.

I get to the front of the barn house when my name is called. Glancing left, I see its Sherman, the band manager. I guess he's done with the groupie he took off with. His timing couldn't be worse.

I reach into my pocket and pull out the money I owe the band. They were great and I plan to hire them again in the future. It seems we have a lot of events coming up we can use them for.

"Thanks, man," I say as I hand the cash over.

"It was an honor, bro. Let us know if you need us again. We can work something out if you want to book regularly."

"Yeah, I'm interested. Look, I need to go but we'll talk about that for sure."

"Oh shit, that building is on fire," Sherman says, causing me to whip my head around.

My heart begins to race as the spa comes into view as smoke bellows from the doors. I snap into action and run for the spa. Jo just ran into that building.

"Call for the fire department," I call back over my shoulder.

I get to the doors, but they are locked. Tearing my shirt off, I use it to try to shake the door open. When that doesn't work, I punch the glass panel and unlock the door.

Once inside, I cover my face. The smoke is filling the place fast. I can barely see.

"Jo, where are—"

I don't fully get my words out before I'm punched in the face. It comes out of nowhere and stuns me a little. Before I know it, I'm being tugged back out of the front door.

Shaking off the shock, I turn to face my attacker. He goes to swing on me again, but I'm ready this time. I duck and toss a right hook hitting him square in the jaw.

He doesn't go down though. I throw another combo before he charges me and knocks me to the ground. We tussle on the ground as our grunts and groans fill the air.

I don't have time for this. I need to get to Jo. Anger fills me and I start to pound on him with my elbow until I knock his hold loose. Quickly, I take the advantage and begin to beat him in the face with my fists.

I can hear Pop barking out orders in the distance, asking for my and Jo's whereabouts. I'm guessing we haven't come into view yet. Suddenly there's a stinging sensation across my chest.

It's not until he tries to slash at my face that I realize he's pulled a blade. I block my face just before he cuts me again. That gives him a chance to push me off him.

I back away quickly and get to my feet. Hershel comes into view out the corner of my eye. He goes to head for me to help as this guy is still swinging the boxcutter in his hand through the air.

"I've got him. Jo and Bell are still inside. Get to my wife and child, Hersh," I bark out.

Hersh stumbles to a stop and nods. I swallow hard. I'm going to make it to my wedding and to see my baby born. This motherfucker isn't going to take everything from us.

"Your wife? Your child? Are you fucking kidding me?" he bellows. "She's fucking pregnant? I had planned to take her back but now she can die in there with that bitch."

"Are you fucking insane?" I growl.

I don't give him time to answer. I send my boot into his chest, causing him to stumble back. While he's winded and gasping, I move in and throw a jab then a right hook.

Blood drops from his mouth, but he won't go down. I'm hitting him hard, I know I am. It's like his crazy is fueling him to stay on his feet.

"I'm going to kill you," he shouts and rushes forward with the blade aimed at me.

I get ready for him. Just as he's about to swing at me, I drop my shoulder and truck him. The move flips him over me and onto his back.

I turn to attack him and make sure he stays down but he reaches out and slashes my leg. I grunt, biting back the pain. He's on his feet again, but I'm not letting up.

I lift my fists ready to keep fighting but the loud sound of a gun going off fills the air and Marty drops to the ground face down. I turn to find Hershel with Bell lying limply in his arms.

Beside them is the woman I love more than life standing with a smoking gun in her hands. Jo is the one who shot Marty. I don't think twice, I limp my way over to her.

Jo tucks the gun away and runs into my arms. I kiss all over her tear-streaked soot covered face. It's never felt this good to have her in my arms.

"Are you all right?"

"I'm okay, but he burned our business down. He ruined our dream," she says sadly.

"As long as you're okay, nothing else matters. We can rebuild. I'll build that place over and over again as long as you're safe."

"There something I need to tell you."

"You're pregnant."

"Yes, I think I am, but I need to tell you about why I think he did this."

I crush my lips to hers. I kiss her with more passion than I think I ever have. We're going to have a baby, nothing else matters to me in this moment.

"I love you so much. Fuck him."

CHAPTER TWENTY-TWO

As It Should Be

Jo

"Do you want me to come in with you?" Chance says as I look out at the coffee shop.

"No, I think this is something I need to do on my own. It will only make it more awkward with you there," I reply as I place a hand on my belly.

At four months, I'm already showing. Between the engagement ring on my finger and the baby bump, I don't think he needs to come inside with me. This is something I need to do alone.

"Okay, I'll be right here if you need me."

"I love you," I say before leaning in to peck him on the lips.

"I love you too. Let's close this chapter once and for all. Yeah?"

"Yeah, see you in a bit."

I climb from the car and dash across the street. I've been wanting to do this since I found out what Marty did. That asshole tried to ruin my life more than once.

I'm still pissed about the rebuild. Thankfully, the spa wasn't completely ruined. It's not a total rebuild, but it is a pain in the ass.

"Hey, Jo," Jarold says as he stands from the table he's waiting at.

"Hey. Thanks for meeting me. I just feel like I need some closure," I say as I take the seat across from him.

"Yeah, I know what you mean. I was happy to hear from you. I mean, I know it's too late for us, obviously," he says, looking pointedly at my little bump. "I just wanted you to know the truth."

"Bell told me everything. I'm so sorry I wouldn't listen to you or give you a chance to explain. It's just I thought you said all you were going to say the day I called."

"I couldn't get into things when you called. I also knew I didn't do anything wrong, so I went back to work like it was nothing because I thought it wasn't.

"I had no idea I was about to lose you. It wasn't until Matthew said something that made me suspicious about Marty that I began to put the pieces together," Jarold says.

"I'm so sorry. I had no idea he was a psycho. We had been friends for years."

"I heard about what happened. Are you okay?"

"Yeah, I'm fine."

"How's Bell? Is your fiancé all right?"

"He's fine. The cuts weren't too deep. He had to get stitches for the leg wound but he's good as new now.

"Bell is still a bit shaken up. She's been staying with my mom while she tries to find a place. I think we're all just glad he's behind bars where he belongs," I say.

"It's fucked up what he did, but I think we're all where we should be. I did love you, Jo. I thought we would be great together, but seeing how happy you are now, I don't know if you ever would have gotten there with me.

"I'm not crazy. I know there was a part of you holding back from me. I don't know if I ever would have gotten through to you.

"I was hurt to lose such an amazing woman, but I think I miss you more as a friend. You don't owe me an apology. Marty might have done you a favor," he chuckles.

Although there's something in his eyes that tells me it's forced. I reach across the table and cover his hand. I do my best to give him a smile.

"I think you're right. Everything is as it should be. I hope you find someone amazing. You're a great guy, Jarold."

"Your dude has found a gem. You keep being amazing. Congratulations on everything. I'll see you next lifetime," he says and winks.

With that, he stands and leans across the table to kiss me on the cheek. He then says goodbye and leaves. I get choked up and a tear slips down my cheek.

I don't turn to watch him go. I needed closure and that's what I have. I don't question the outcome of what has happened.

Chance is the one for me. I just hate how Marty affected all our lives. It was wrong and Chance nor Jarold deserved how Marty's actions changed their lives.

I know Chance will be fine. He's been pushing the rebuild and making sure things remain on track. I think he's been enjoying the time we get to work together at the inn and brewery instead.

Our lives will be just fine. Knowing firsthand the lasting effects trauma can have, I can only hope Jarold finds his peace in all of this. I know I'm not a jinx, but this did come from me and that lies heavily on my conscious.

"How are you feeling? Did you get what you needed?"

I look up to find Chance sitting where Jarold had been. I smile and tilt my head to the side. I should have known he wasn't going to stay in the car.

"I thought you were going to wait for me."

"I saw him leave and you've been sitting here staring off into space. I wanted to come in and make sure you were okay."

"I'm fine. Thank you for coming to check in on me. Yeah, I got what I needed."

"He doesn't blame you like I said, right?"

"No, he doesn't blame me. He said something that rang true."

"Oh yeah, what's that?"

"Everything is as it should be."

"That it is, baby. We're about to go meet with your dad about our wedding. You're having our first baby and you're right where you belong. In Spring Valley making beer with me."

"All things that are true," I sing.

"Let's go. I want to get one of those sandwiches from that place by the house."

"Oh my God, you have to have one of those every time we come to the city now," I laugh.

I look at him lovingly. I'm not going to complain because I've been craving the same thing. I was hoping we could make the stop.

"Best thing here." He gives me a wink and stands to take my hand.

CHAPTER TWENTY-THREE

Family

Jack

I bounce my adorable little granddaughter in my arms as I watch my son fidget with his tie. I can feel his nervous energy from across the room. I tear up as I think of the days when he was this small.

I used to hold him in my arms and sniff his tiny head just like this. Where does time go? One minute they need you for everything, the next they have their own family and they're teaching you all the things the world has changed around you and you don't understand.

I'm so proud of Chance. April begins to whimper, breaking into my thoughts. I open my eyes and look down at her.

"Hey, my sweet darlin'. What's the matter?"

"Ah, ah," she coos.

"Your daddy does look sharp," I coo back. "You're proud of him too, aren't you? Yes, you are."

"I can take her, Pop," Hershel offers.

"You think I don't know how to take care of my own granddaughter?"

"Pop, I'm just trying to help."

"You can get your practice in some other time. This little angel is staying right here with her Paw-paw."

"Pop, I could use your help with this tie. I can't seem to get it right."

I sigh and turn to head over to Chance, not giving up my hold on April. I love being a grandfather. Today is a proud day for me and Coral. Our babies are getting married.

This day feels almost a good as the day April was born. It's one thing to be there for the birth of your own offspring. It's another to see their child born. It's like confirmation of all the things you've done right.

"You know you're spoiling her, don't you?"

"I'm her grandfather, that's my job."

"You can't fix my tie with her in your arms, Pop."

"Why the hell not? When you have two of your own and they're both old enough to put a tie on or help someone else to, then you can tell me what I can and can't do with a baby in my arms.

"Heck, I used to hold Hersh in my arms while changing your stinking diapers. Now hush." I smile. "You're getting married today."

"Ah," April squeals.

"See, my little darlin' agrees."

Chance chuckles and holds his hands up. "All right, all right. Let's get to it. My girl is waiting for me. How do I look?"

"Like you're about to walk the red carpet. Your mama would be so proud. I love you, son."

"I love you too, Pop. I couldn't have done any of this without you."

Jo

"Man, the women in this family make some pretty ass brides," Mel sings from her perch on the couch as she sits with a glass in her hand.

"I know, right? I thought Mom looked amazing at her wedding. Jo, you're glowing," JC says.

"Thanks, guys. I'm so nervous."

"You're going to be fine. Chance has been waiting for this day longer than you know. Everything is going to be just as we planned. Your father spared no expense for your special day. We're both so proud of you," Mom coos.

"Ugh, but my breasts are so swollen and I swear I'm going to leak all over my gown. We should have given it some more time," I murmur.

"For what? You would just have two babies under one if you had," JC says then grunts as Mel elbows her.

"Wait, what? I didn't tell—"

"Girl, welcome to Spring Valley," Mel sings and shrugs.

CHAPTER TWENTY-FOUR

What Happened

Jodie Cadence

Tears cling to my lashes as I look up at Hershel. I have so much I want to say but none of it seems right. He's become so much more to me than someone trying to help me out of a jam.

He's no longer the annoying guy trying to impress me. I see so much more in Hershel than I did when I first came to this town. Yet here I am about to lose the most important relationship I've allowed myself outside of family in years.

"Hershel, please let me explain."

"You have nothing you need to explain. After all, none of it was real, right?"

"Wrong," I choke out hating how angry he sounds. "You know me better than anyone. You have to know—"

"Jodie, they need us," David says interrupting us.

Hershel pulls a hand down his face and nods. "You owe me nothing. I'll see you around."

"Hershel, Hershel," I call after him.

I ball my fists and close my eyes. My heart crumbles and I want to sink to the floor. I had everything I wanted.

"Jodie, you're needed now."

I turn to head out to where I'm needed. However, not before I walk pass David. It takes everything in me not to lunge at him.

"You smug prick. I'm not done with you. You're going to pay for this," I snarl as I walk by and bump him hard.

How did this get so fucked up?

ABOUT THE AUTHOR

Blue Saffire, award-winning, bestselling author of over eighty contemporary romance novels and novellas, writes with the intention to touch the heart and the mind. Blue hooks, weaves, and loops multiple series, keeping you engaged in her worlds. Blue writes for her own publishing company, Perceptive Illusions as Blue Saffire, as well as Royal Blue.

Blue and her husband live in a house filled with laughter and creativity in Long Island, NY. Both working hard to build the Blue brand and cultivate their love for the arts. Creative is their family affair.

Blue holds an MBA in Marketing and Project Management, as well as an MED in Instructional Technology and Curriculum Design. She is also an NLP Master Practitioner.

ORPHAN **HOLD**
DO NOT SHIP

H1 – 000000000267

ISBN 9781941924372

CLIENT	Alternate Sourcing
STATION	TPP Receiving Station 03
HELD	2026 – 10 – 08 08:53

SHELF

If its order arrives, scan this label at a receiving station.

ACKNOWLEDGMENTS

Ah, that was fun. I think we brush off trauma that comes from childhood. Not everyone heals or even realizes they need to heal. That's what I loved about Jo. She did the work. No, it wasn't pretty or easy, but she did it and got her happy ending.

We're halfway through the Spring Valley world. JC and Mel are going to bring us more love, laughter, and answers. I can't wait.

My dear reader friends, I can't go without saying thank you so much for your continued support and patience. More is to come.

Thank you for the encouraging reviews, emails, videos, posts, shares, comments, and DMs. Big thanks, friends. Remember, sharing is caring. If you have a friend who reads, let them know about me, please and thank you.

Hey big head, thanks for being there for another one. I'm still laughing at your reaction to Chance's fight. Thank you for being my partner in crime and my sounding board. Love you to life and beyond.

As always, all thanks to my source. God has breathed a purpose into me, and I'm focused on making it happen. I remain grateful and locked in. To God be all the Glory.

This is where passion meets fire. Thank you, Lord, thank you.

Next! Let's find out what's going on with JC and Hershel.

Wait, there is more to come! You can stay updated with my latest releases, learn more about me, the author, and be a part of contests by subscribing to my newsletter at

www.BlueSaffire.com

If you enjoyed *Beer with Me*, I'd love to hear

your thoughts and please feel free to leave a

review on my website. And when you do, please let me

know by emailing me TheBlueSaffire@gmail.com

or leave a comment on Facebook https://www.facebook.com/BlueSaffireDiaries or Twitter @TheBlueSaffire

Other books by Blue Saffire

Placed in Best Reading Order

Also available ...

Legally Bound

Legally Bound 2: Against the Law

Legally Bound 3: His Law

Perfect for Me

Hush 1: Family Secrets

Ballers: His Game

Brothers Black 1: Wyatt the Heartbreaker

Legally Bound 4: Allegations of Love

Hush 2: Slow Burn

Legally Bound 5.0: Sam

Yours 1: Losing My Innocence

Yours 2: Experience Gained

Yours 3: Life Mastered

Ballers 2: His Final Play

Legally Bound 5.1: Tasha Illegal Dealings

Brothers Black 2: Noah

Legally Bound 5.2: Camille

Legally Bound 5.3 & 5.4 Special Edition

Where the Pieces Fall

Legally Bound 5.5: Legally Unbound

Brothers Black 4: Braxton the Charmer

Broken Soldier

Brothers Black 5: Felix the Watcher

A Home for Christmas

Doctor Feel Good

Brothers Black 6: Ryan the Joker

Brothers Black 7: Johnathan the Fixer

Wild Hearts

Pieces of Trevor's Heart

Ballers 3: His Team

Ronan Book 1: Kings of New York

Dylan Book 2: Kings of New York

Coming Soon…

King of Gods Book 4: Immortal Iron Brothers Series
King of Past Book 5: Immortal Iron Brothers Series
Brooklyn Book 3: Kings of New York Series

Other Blue Saffire Series

Hold On To Me Series

My Funny Valentine
Be My Valentine

Hitter Squad Series

Remember Me

Work Husband Series

Unexpected Lovers
My Best Friend's Wish
The Ones Left Behind
The Last Ones Standing

The Lost Souls MC Series

Forever
Never
Always

The Moran Brothers Series

Love Notes
Stay With Me

The Ahole Club Series**

Pit Book 1: The A**hole Club
Ox Book 5: The A**hole Club
Kelex Book 6: The A**hole Club

Immortal Iron Brothers Series

King of Knights Book 1
King of Inferno Book 2
King of Tides Book 3

Check out Blue Saffire exclusives on the
BlueSaffire.com website
The Fixer
His Miracle Baby

Dark Disciples Series
Razor
Dane
Trip

Discipline Disciples Series
Wounded
12 Rounds

Bay Breezes Series
Professor Jones
Room 112

Love's Brew Series
Heart to Heart
Beer With Me
Clouded Views coming soon …

Other books from Evei Lattimore Collection Books by Blue Saffire
Black Bella 1

Destiny 1: Life Decisions
Destiny 2: Decisions of the Next Generation
Destiny 3 coming soon…

Star

Other books from Royal Blue Gay Romance Collection written by Blue Saffire
Kyle's Reveal
Beau's Redemption

www.ingramcontent.com/pod-product-compliance
Lightning Source LLC
Chambersburg PA
CBHW061555250926
52052CB00010B/3214
9781941924372